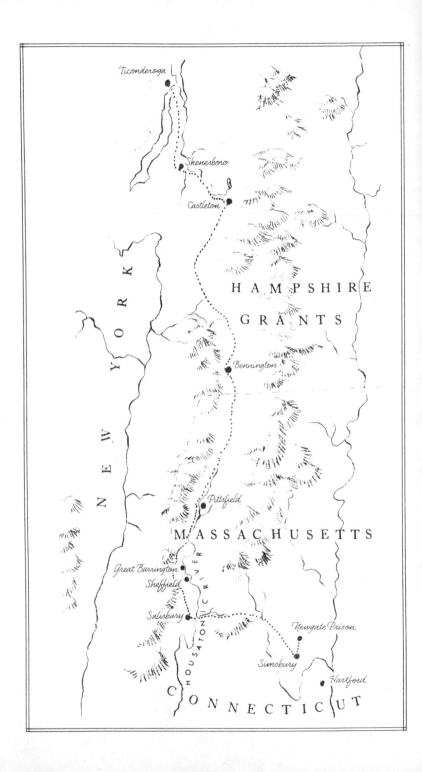

A Spy at TICONDEROGA

By Clavin Fisher

Illustrated by
Jeanne Johns

BERKSHIRE TRAVELLER PRESS
Stockbridge, Massachusetts 01262

SELECTED TITLES FROM
THE BERKSHIRE TRAVELLER PRESS

Once Told Tales

FIRST ENCOUNTER SERIES:
The Indian and the White Man
    in Connecticut
The Indian and the White Man
    in Massachussetts & Rhode Island

Fourth Printing

Fisher, Clavin, 1912—
    A Spy at Ticonderoga.

    SUMMARY: After convincing his uncle to take him along on the expedi-
tion to capture Ticonderoga, a fourteen-year-old orphan plays an important
part in making the campaign a success.

    1. Ticonderoga, N.Y.—History—Capture, 1775—Juvenile fiction. [1. Ti-
conderoga, N.Y.—History—Capture, 1775—Fiction. 2. United States—History —Revolution,1775-1783 —Fiction] I. Johns, Jeanne. II. Title.

PZ7.F1996Sp   [Fic]   75-14203
ISBN 0-912944-30-7

Copyright © 1975 Berkshire Traveller Press

To
Wendy and Peter
who have listened to my tales
of history with patience and fortitude.

FOREWORD

A Spy at Ticonderoga is a story of the adventures of a 14-year-old youth with the expedition to capture Fort Ticonderoga from the British in the spring of 1775.

The story features interesting historical facts about the expedition that haven't been general knowledge. For example, the Ticonderoga expedition started from Hartford and Simsbury, Conn., and was conceived, planned and financed by the Connecticut Committee of Safety.

Ethan Allen's success was due in no small part to three Connecticut militia officers: Col. Benedict Arnold who shared command with Allen at the time of the assault; Capt. Edward Mott of New Preston, Conn., who led the expedition until it reached the Hampshire Grants (Vermont); and, Capt. Noah Phelps of Simsbury, Conn., who spied on the fort in advance of the attack.

All of the major events in the story associated with the adult characters took place as depicted.

CONTENTS

1. The Mysterious Horseman

David Holcomb first noticed the horseman as he arose from his spot on the bank of the river. That's a dumb, dangerous speed to come down a mountain, he thought, watching a cloud of dust rise as the rider urged his mount down Weatogue Mountain. Somebody must be in a powerful passion to get to Simsbury.

Picking up his canteen, he fingered the coiled rattle-snake painted in red on the wooden surface. "Don't tread on me!" he whispered, tracing the words beneath the snake.

As he gathered his copy book and pencils, he examined the sketch of the river he had just completed. Not bad, he thought, but the water looked a little funny.

David shouldered his canteen and ambled across the spring-green meadow toward his uncle's house of unpainted clapboards, set alone against the mountain. The late April sun added a touch of color to the Phelps' house and bathed meadow, field and river in a soft golden sheen.

He stopped to admire the view of mountain and valley. It must be the prettiest spot in the whole Connecticut Colony, he thought. He felt an easing of the pain for the first time since that terrible day in Concord two weeks ago. The tight, hurt feeling came only at intervals now.

Reaching the newly ploughed strip, he thrust a bare foot into the soil, enjoying the warmth and pleasure of smashing clods of dirt with his toes. He poked about for arrowheads, remembering the ones he had found yesterday as he ploughed with Cousin Matthew. Matt told him that the Massacoh tribe had its summer village on this site a hundred years ago.

Movement caught his eye again and his blue eyes narrowed as he squinted at the horseman who had reached level ground and appeared to be heading for Uncle Noah's house. Maybe he's come from Concord or Lexington to report more fighting, David thought, his curiosity rising. But then, the horseman could have come from Hartford on the other side of Weatogue Mountain.

David reached for his canteen. He pulled the plug, tilted it and drank, water dribbling down his square-set chin onto his gray linsey-woolsey shirt. He wiped his chin with the back of his hand and dried his hand on his buff-colored breeches. With a toss of his head he tumbled his long blond hair from his face and proceeded toward home.

He would have to call Uncle Noah's house "home" now. But memories of his father's house in Concord kept crowding in at times. Slowly he was warming up to Simsbury as his adopted town and to the Phelps as his adopted parents.

Suddenly the horseman came into full view at a brisk canter, his cocked hat bobbing and saddle bags flapping. David shuddered, recalling that awful night when a horseman awakened him in Concord with the cry, "The British are coming! To arms!"

The old hurt in his chest returned as he remembered only too clearly the sharp sound of shooting at the bridge. Then came the sober detachment of Concord militiamen carrying his father home and laying him gently on the bedstead. He would be forever indebted to Uncle Noah who arrived from Connecticut with the Simsbury militia and helped bury his father.

After the funeral he was reluctant to accept Noah's invitation to come to Simsbury to live with the Phelps. How could he leave a home that held so many reminders of his father and the great times they had had together?

His eyes stung as he remembered the winter evenings in the kitchen before the great fire. He couldn't avoid his nightly school lessons because his father was schoolmaster but after each lesson they shared an "adventure hour." It might be reading the exploits of Ulysses or Tom Jones or seeing who could make the best sketch of the fireplace and utensils.

Several neighbors offered David a home but Noah insisted that the Phelps always take care of their own. So quietly and sadly David sorted out his most prized posessions from a roomful of treasures. He could take only what he could carry on his back for it was a four-day march to Simsbury with Noah and the militia. This meant leaving behind his fishing pole and many of his best sketches of Concord. Noah did let him take his father's military canteen, for that would be useful on the journey. It had seemed like a long march to David. Each step was taking him away from all the things he knew and loved and with every mile his resentment of the British grew a little stronger.

David was jolted back to the present by the arrival of the horseman at the Phelps house. The stranger tossed the reins to Cousin Matthew who had burst through the front door.

"I must see Captain Phelps immediately," the stranger shouted. Leaping from his horse, the man strode to the door where he was greeted by Uncle Noah.

Excited by this action, David broke into a trot. He watched with amusement as Matt tried to follow the stranger through the front door, only to be ordered out. Matt turned and approached David, an expression of frustration clouding his round, freckled face.

"What's it all about?" David shouted to his young cousin.

Matt shrugged his shoulders. "Who knows! King George might be dead for all I know."

David laughed. "I don't think there'd be any reason to keep that a secret."

Suddenly Matt grabbed David's arm. "My father asked us to thin out the lilacs, didn't he?"

"Of course—so what?"

Matt spun around and raced for the tool shed, leaving David puzzled. Matt was back within seconds, a spade over his shoulder. He put a finger to his lips and advanced on tiptoes to the parlor window. David followed, suddenly grasping Matt's plan.

"I think we can hear'em!" Matt whispered, leaning on the spade and listening intently.

David strained to sort out words from the jumbled

conversation coming from the parlor. All of a sudden the
stranger's voice came clearly as he said with determina-
tion, "Then it's agreed! In two day's you'll get your
brother Elisha and we'll start for Ticonderoga. By the
kindness of Providence we'll have those cannon and we'll
drag them to Cambridge and blow the British out of
Boston!"

David leaned against the house. His hands shook and
his scalp prickled with excitement. He grasped Matt by
the shoulders. "I'm going on that expedition. They can't
refuse me even if I'm only fourteen. I'm going to get
even for what the British did to my father!"

2. David Strikes a Bargain

David stood beside Matt at the long table with the white linen broad cloth. The pewter plates glowed softly in the candlelight. He looked across at the freckled face and impatient green eyes of 11-year-old Roxy, noticing how much she looked like her 13-year-old brother.

Uncle Noah finished his long grace that seemed like a sermon to David and motioned the children to be seated. David sat down and stole a glance at the stranger with his fine blue waistcoat, starched linen collar and handsome rugged face.

David itched to find out the details of the expedition to Ticonderoga. But he knew better than to ask any questions. Uncle Noah wouldn't tolerate questions from the children at the table any more than he would let them sit during grace. David found this hard to take as he and his father had talked freely togeher at meals about a wide range of interesting topics. But then his father had always encouraged questions from the children he was teaching.

Aunt Lydia brought in pewter chargers of ham and steaming greens. David's tankard was filled and refilled with milk. The candles shrank into their holders, but David was hardly conscious of eating. The conversation drifted from the dreadful spring drought to the scarcity of seed without causing a ripple in David's thoughts. In his mind he was storming the walls of Fort Ticonderoga and capturing a redcoat after a wild heroic struggle.

The stranger, who turned out to be a Captain Mott

from Hartford, departed following a whispered conversation with Noah at the front door. Aunt Lydia sent Matt and Roxy up the stairs to bed. David saw his chance and approached Uncle Noah.

"May I see you, sir, for a few minutes?" David said, his heart racing.

Uncle Noah looked at David, his eyes narrowing, and replied, "Of course, Davey. Let's go into the parlor." He picked up a candle from the dining room and led David into the next room.

Choosing a rocking chair, David faced his uncle who had elected the settle. David inspected his uncle, trying to guess what kind of a mood he was in. The candlelight revealed Noah's strong handsome face, blue eyes, bushy eyebrows and full brown hair. It told nothing of what he was thinking.

"I have a request to make," David blurted. "I—"

"Is something wrong, Davey?" Noah interrupted. "Have we been unkind or—"

It was David's turn to interrupt. "No. You've been just great to me." He drew a deep breath. "It isn't that. I want to go with you to Ticonderoga."

David held his breath as he watched surprise register on his uncle's face.

"How did you know we plan to go to Ticonderoga?" Noah asked quietly, his expression becoming severe.

"Matt and I were thinning the lilacs—like you said we should — and we heard Captain Mott telling you about the expedition."

"That was a mighty convenient place to be at that particular moment," Noah said, a touch of sarcasm in his voice. "But listen Davey, you're only fourteen. You have to be sixteen for the militia."

"I'll be fifteen in a few months," David replied, hoping

Noah wouldn't ask how many months that would be. "Besides, Father told me you ran away from home when you were a boy and helped General Amherst capture Fort Ticonderoga from the French in 1759."

David searched Noah's face, hoping to see agreement. Instead, he watched it break into a frown.

"Listen, Davey," Noah replied softly, "I was seventeen when I joined the militia in the French and Indian War — not fourteen like you. Your mother was my sister and when she died at your birth, your Aunt Lydia and I felt some responsibility for you even while your father was alive. Now that he's—gone, we have double responsibility. I can't let you go on the expedition to Fort Ti."

David sagged in the rocker, fighting for control of his emotions. Suddenly he straightened up and with a quivering lip cried, "But Uncle Noah, I've got to get a British soldier to get even for the redcoat who killed my Father!"

"So that's how it is," Noah murmured, getting up and rumpling David's hair. "Listen, Davey. If you want to serve the colonies I've got a job for you. Fighting redcoats isn't the only way to win a war."

"I don't want your old job!" David said defiantly. "I want to go to Ticonderoga!"

Noah returned to the settle slowly. "Davey, this job is very important. If completed, it might make the difference between success or failure at Ticonderoga."

Afraid he might have gone too far, David remained silent.

Noah continued. "Last week our Committee of Safety received a report that one of our Simsbury men, Jim Sneir, had been to Fort Ti. We suspect he's a Tory. When he passed through here on his way to New York, probably to report to the British, we captured him—but he won't talk."

"What could I do?" David inquired, puzzled at how this affected him.

"Well," Noah replied, "up to now I didn't much care whether he talked or not. We just wanted to keep him from reporting to the British. But now with our expedition to capture Ticonderoga, I must find out from him the strength of the garrison at the fort. We've got to know what we're going to be up against."

"You mean you think I could make him talk?"

Noah smiled. "It depends on how good an actor you are."

"What do you mean?"

Noah leaned forward, looking at David intently, his eyes shining in the candlelight. "Sneir won't talk to any of our Simsbury men. We've tried. He sits in that old copper mine we've turned into a prison and doesn't say a word. He knows we're all against the King. But he doesn't know you. You could make out you're a Tory and for King George."

David rocked back and forth, excitement rising. Perhaps he could make believe he and his father had been chased out of Concord as Tories. He winced at that, wondering what his father would have thought of that lie. Then he got a sudden inspiration.

"Uncle Noah," David said eagerly, "if I do this — and if I'm successful — can I go with you to Ticonderoga?"

David watched Noah's jaw drop. He held his breath as Noah looked at the floor and sighed.

After an interval Noah said quietly, "All right, Davey, you've struck a bargain."

3. The Road to Newgate Prison

David strapped his knapsack to his back, slung his canteen over his left shoulder, and stepped out into the chill wind. Mountainous white clouds brightened the blue sky. He was glad of the deerskin jacket Uncle Noah had loaned him.

Uncle Noah came out of the barn, carrying a leather pail of milk and shouted, "I'm sorry I couldn't let you have a horse. They're all needed for ploughing. We've got to get much of our seed in before I leave."

David sighed at Noah's, "before I leave." He doesn't expect me to succeed at the prison and go with him to Ticonderoga, he thought. I'm afraid he's right. I don't see how I'm going to get that old Tory to talk.

Noah continued. "Davey, just follow this road north. Don't take any turns. Always keep Weatogue Mountain on your right. It's about ten miles."

"What's the prison like?" David asked.

"It's not much. The prisoners are kept underground, in the mine, during the night. In the daytime they cut wood and perform other chores in an enclosure above ground. The note I gave you for Captain Viets will get you into the prison. I'm sure he'll have a bed for you in his house for the night."

"For the night? What about the other nights?"

"Didn't I tell you that you have to be back tomorrow night? Let's see, today is Wednesday, April 26th. You've got to be back tomorrow because I leave for Ticonderoga on Friday."

David winced at the "I leave" again. The whole business did seem so hopeless, anyway. How could he possibly get Sneir to talk in so short a time?

Noah's ringing "good luck" echoed off Weatogue Mountain as David started north at a rapid pace. He might as well get there as fast as possible.

The day seemed typical for late April. One minute the sun was out and he felt like peeling off his jacket. The next minute it was under a cloud and the wind felt as if it had just come from the North Pole.

He stopped to admire a patch of coltsfoot violets, wishing he had brought his copybook with him. He wanted to sketch the flowers but there wasn't time. Anyway, the only person that really liked his drawings was Cousin Roxy.

At least the walk was fun, he thought. He enjoyed the spring countryside, the jangle of cowbells, bluebirds back again, a hawk cruising in the sky, and all around him the fresh earthy smell of spring.

He was about to stop for a drink from his canteen when he saw a horseman approaching. Curiosity kept him walking.

As the rider drew near, David observed his unusual clothes. Everything he wore was of leather, from his floppy hat, leather shirt and breeches to his leather leggings and shoes. His enormous leather saddlebags bulged mysteriously.

"Ha!" exclaimed David to himself. "I know what this character is even if I never saw one before. I bet he's a traveling cobbler."

The rider reined in and peered down at David, his fat sunburned face breaking into a smile.

"Good morning, sir," David greeted, and then not knowing what else to say, he blurted out, without thinking, "How's business?"

"Well, my young friend," the stranger answered, "I might ask you the same question except I'd consider it rude."

David reddened.

"But since you've asked, I don't mind telling you. It's very good. I've just come from Newgate Prison where I had a contract to make a dozen pairs of shoes for the prisoners. Cheap shoes, though. Captain Viets drives a hard bargain."

"Newgate Prison!" David cried. "What's it like there!?"

"I'll tell you this, young man. I'll never go down into that mine with those rascals. They're a mean lot. Captain Viets wanted me to go down to fit shoes to one who was sick. I refused. He might have slit my throat, for all you know."

David gulped.

"Well, have a good walk," the cobbler cried as he nudged his horse down the road.

A chill settled over David. He tightened the thongs of his jacket.

The day didn't seem pleasant anymore. Nor did his journey. He plodded along mechanically, putting one foot in front of the other. He passed several farmhouses and crossroads without really seeing them.

Feeling hungry, David remembered the chicken and

biscuits Aunt Lydia had put in his knapsack. He found shelter from the wind in a convenient thicket and un-hitched his knapsack and canteen. A few bites of the well-seasoned chicken made him feel a little better.

He looked at his canteen with the coiled snake and the motto. Happy memories of his father overwhelmed him. He remembered the great hikes together, the fun of the first snowflake in winter and the first violet in spring. And then there were the exciting meetings of the Concord Committee of Safety when his father so elo-quently denounced the latest British tax.

Brushing away tears that started to form, David pounded a fist into his knapsack. He would get revenge on those rotten Lobsterbacks!

Setting a brisk pace, he soon spotted what surely must be Newgate Prison. Ahead on his left was a large clear-ing in the forest. A barn-like structure sat in the middle of it, surrounded by high walls of fieldstone, topped by wooden pickets. It all looked a bit grim.

With renewed apprehension, David walked slower, heading for a farmhouse opposite the prison. Reaching the front door, he banged the brass knocker. The door opened and a gruff voice invited him in.

4. Tory Sneir

Captain Viets stood on his doorstep shaking his head. He was a tall man with a straight, military appearance, square chin and close-cropped graying hair.

"I don't understand your Uncle Noah," Viets said. "We've tried for two weeks to get Sneir to tell us what he was doing at Ticonderoga. We've even threatened to tar and feather him and ride him out of town. How does Noah expect you to make him talk?"

David hesitated. Uncle Noah had warned him that no one was to know about the proposed expedition to Ticonderoga—not even Captain Viets.

"I guess it was as much my idea as Uncle Noah's," David said, with a glance at the high walls of Newgate. "I thought that since I'm not from Simsbury and Sneir doesn't know me, I could make believe I'm a Tory. I could tell him my father and I were run out of Concord."

"Even if he believes," Viets said, "that's not necessarily any reason for him to volunteer to tell you why he was at Fort Ticonderoga." Viets paused and shrugged his shoulders. "But there's no harm in trying."

Viets called through the doorway and his wife soon appeared with food for Sneir. Viets handed David a battered charger of stew and a tankard of cider.

"We've kept Sneir in the mine twenty-four hours a day, hoping that'll make him talk," Viets said.

David gasped, remembering what the cobbler had said about going down into the mine.

"The guard will tell you how to find Sneir. Wait for Sneir to finish eating and bring back the utensils. I can't have him or anyone else making knives out of my pewter."

Viets turned abruptly and went into the house. David walked slowly across the road to the prison gate, carrying the charger and tankard. His stomach tensed at the thought of going down in the mine. Balancing both utensils on one arm, he pulled a bell rope that hung over the wall. A bell clanged.

An unshaven face leered at him through a peephole. Bloodshot eyes focused on the food David held. A bolt was thrown and the gate opened.

David felt himself at the center of a stage. A dozen prisoners stopped their loitering to stare at him with looks of sullen curiosity. He was shocked by their unshaven, unhealthy appearance and filthy, tattered clothes.

A voice at his elbow said, "If you're taking grub to Sneir, you'd better get moving or someone else will take it away from you."

David turned and looked into the face from the peephole. Obviously this was the guard, he thought, because he was carrying a musket. But he didn't look any better than the prisoners.

"Follow me," the guard commanded.

Staring straight ahead to avoid the eyes of the prisoners, David followed the guard into a shed. The feeble light from a lantern revealed a round hole in the center of the dirt floor from which the end of a ladder protruded.

The guard pointed to the ladder. He looked at David, his expression implying, "You got the guts to go down there?"

David walked over to the ladder and looked down into the hole. He gasped and drew back as he was hit by an awful odor rising from the mine.

The guard laughed. "It don't smell pretty down there but they gets used to it. When you get to the bottom of the ladder, take the left shaft. You'll see Sneir's light toward the end of the shaft. He's the only one in that section of the mine. Here, you need a light."

The guard took the lantern off a peg and hung it around David's neck. The warmth felt good. Then the guard gave a low laugh and shuffled out of the shed.

David cradled the charger of stew to his chest and hooked his fingers into the tankard of cider. He placed a foot on the ladder and grabbed the top rung with his right hand. The odor was suffocating. He closed his eyes and held on until the dizziness passed.

Looking down, he saw nothing but a few feet of the ladder. The faint light from the lantern wouldn't penetrate any farther. He twisted his head away from the hole and drew in a deep breath of fresh air. Holding his breath he took one step down—and another.

Five steps down he could hold his breath no longer. He let it out with a sigh and drew a quick short breath.

It was like sucking in fumes from a witches kettle. He felt dizzy again but he held tight to the ladder with his right hand and closed his eyes. Fortunately the charger and tankard remained upright.

He experimented with quick short breaths and finally decided he could tolerate the odor. He looked up longingly at the round hole of light above. Then he gritted his teeth and descended, the circle of light above slowly closing to a pin hole.

At last his light revealed the stone floor of the mine and in a few more steps he found himself in a tunnel. The air was damp. Only the sound of dripping water disturbed a great silence. A drop of icy water hit his neck and he shivered.

Walking cautiously forward he found the floor of the tunnel slimy, uneven and treacherous. The dark, wet walls glistened in the rays of light from his lantern.

Suddenly he faced a blank wall as the tunnel ended, with branches to the left and right. Remembering the guard's instructions, he turned left and was relieved to see a faint light down the tunnel. But as he drew near the light his fear returned. What was Tory Sneir like?

He soon found out. In a little alcove off the tunnel, a man lay sleeping on a mat of straw. He was covered by a torn gray blanket. An open book by a flickering candle indicated he had fallen asleep while reading.

David set the charger and tankard on the floor and stared at the sleeping prisoner. He squatted on the floor and glanced around the alcove, stopping short at iron rings in the ceiling. He had heard prisoners sometimes were chained by their wrists to rings like this. He was glad Sneir wasn't.

Then his eyes traveled back to Sneir and he gasped as he saw that the Tory's ankles were chained to rings in the stone floor. Sneir opened his eyes and sat up.

"Who are you?" the Tory demanded.

David looked at the bearded face, straggly gray hair and reddened eyes, fear turning to sympathy. The blanket had fallen from Sneir, revealing an expensive blue waistcoat and yellow breeches, both badly stained and wrinkled.

"Speak up, boy!" the Tory demanded. "Who are you?"

"David Holcomb. I've been hired to bring you food and do other things about the prison."

Sneir saw the food for the first time and held out his hands for it. David watched as the Tory gulped the cider and eagerly dug into the heavy dark stew with his fingers.

After using the blanket to wipe his hands and face, the Tory put the blanket down and stared at David. David squirmed, feeling ashamed that any man should be chained up in so miserable a fashion.

"You don't look like one of those crazy Liberty Boys with hair as long as a wild Indian's," the Tory said, his face screwing up in disgust.

Here it comes, David thought. I've got to play-act now.

"No, sir," David said. "I'm not a Liberty Boy. I'm for the king."

"Then what are you doing here? This stinkin' Simsbury is no place for a lad loyal to the Crown."

David looked down at the floor while he attempted to create a sorrowful expression on his face. Turning to Sneir he said sadly, "I'm not from Simsbury, sir. I'm from Concord in Massachusetts. While I was visiting here, my father was tarred and feathered and run out of Concord because he favors the king. My mother is dead. I'm earning my keep by working for Captain Viets."

David watched Sneir's face for a hint as to whether his story was being believed. He saw no change of expression.

Trying a bold approach, David said, "I understand you've been to Ticonderoga. It must be real exciting there. What's it like?"

Sneir gave a start and frowned. "You, too?" he said sadly. "Everyone keeps prodding me about Ticonderoga."

"I don't understand," David lied. "Why should anyone be so interested in what you saw there?"

"You wouldn't understand," Sneir said.

David's hopes sank. He couldn't continue the conversation about Ticonderoga without arousing Sneir's suspicion. He changed the subject.

"You must have read that book several times," he said. "Would you like me to get you another?"

"I don't need another book half as much as I need a razor," Sneir said, running his fingers through his beard. "I'd be indebted to you, lad, if you'd get me a razor, soap and a mirror."

"I'll try my best," David said, gathering up the empty charger and tankard. "I'll be back tomorrow."

"You're a good boy," Sneir called out as David retreated down the tunnel.

5. The Tory's Letter

David sat on the stone slab by Captain Viet's front door surveying the prison with his head between his hands. How could he possibly get Sneir to talk about Ticonderoga? Today was his second and last chance. Noah said he was leaving for the fort tomorrow. It began to look as if Noah and Elisha would be going without him.

Captain Viets came out, carrying the charger and tankard. "I sent the soap, razor and mirror down to Sneir by the guard this morning," he said. "You couldn't carry that and the food, too."

David sighed, too discouraged with events to comment. He could imagine Noah and the men storming the parapets at Ticonderoga, with the British cowering in their quarters. What he wouldn't give to go along on the expedition.

"I can't imagine why Sneir wants to shave," Viets continued. "He isn't going anywhere. And he doesn't need to look into a mirror to shave. I sent him only a broken piece of mirror glass."

David hardly heard Viets, his mind still on Ticonderoga. He took the charger and tankard and shuffled over to the gate. He pulled the bell rope and the same bleary eyes peered at him through the peephole.

This time David took little notice of the guard and prisoners. He followed the guard to the shed and cradled the tankard and charger in one arm while the guard slung the lantern around his neck. Reaching the ladder, his stomach contracted as the odor hit him. Steeling himself, he descended.

Approaching the light along the left tunnel, he saw Sneir quickly crumple a piece of paper at the sound of his approach. The Tory then held another piece of paper over his candle.

"It's so damp down here my letter is wet," Sneir explained.

David was surprised by Sneir's changed appearance. With his beard off, the Tory was handsome, despite his hollow cheeks and watery eyes. David wondered just what made Sneir a Tory, anyway. He didn't look any different than any farmer or merchant in Simsbury or Concord. In fact he looked a lot better than many of the roughnecks who paraded with banners through the streets of Boston, shouting foul things at the British.

"How would you like to earn a shilling?" the Tory asked, looking at David inquisitively.

This is a switch, David thought. What's he up to anyway? I've got to play this carefully.

"I wouldn't mind," David replied, "as long as it won't cost me my job."

Sneir smiled. "It won't. All I want you to do is see that this letter I've written gets to Hartford—to the driver of the stage coach to New York. Here's a shilling for you and one for the driver." The Tory took two silver coins from his vest pocket and handed them to David.

David's heart jumped. Maybe this letter would be telling someone about Ticonderoga!

Fighting to steady his voice, David said, "I'll be glad

to see that your letter gets to the driver of the New York stage."

"Good boy," Sneir said, folding the paper and inserting it in an envelope. Fumbling through another vest pocket, he extracted a short stick of brown sealing wax. He held the wax over the candle until several drops of sealing wax fell on the flap of the envelope. Carefully he pressed a large signet ring into the soft wax. With a pencil from his pocket he addressed the envelope.

David watched, entranced. What luck! The letter delivered to Noah ought to assure his going to Ticonderoga!

Sneir looked at David intently. "I wouldn't tell Captain Viets about this letter."

"Of course not," David replied. "It's none of his business."

"Good boy," the Tory murmured; then added, "Will you get a chance to get into Hartford soon?"

"Yes," David lied. "In fact Captain Viets said I could go there with a guard tomorrow. We are picking up some new prisoners there sent by the army in Cambridge."

"Splendid, splendid. I'm very anxious that this letter goes as fast as possible. By the way, do you know the purpose of my letter?"

David rocked back on his heels, startled. "Why—no. I have no idea."

Sneir smiled. "It's about you."

"Me!" David exclaimed. "I don't understand."

"I can't see a bright boy like you, especially one loyal to the Crown, waiting on prisoners in a stinkin' rat hole like this." Sneir looked around at the damp, slimy walls and wrinkled his nose. "I'm writing a friend in New York, asking him to get you a decent job. What do you think of that, boy?"

David's jaw dropped. He forced a smile to hide the

bitter frustration that churned inside him.

The Tory reached out and touched David's knee. "That's all right, boy. I see by your face how much you would like to get rid of this job. We'll soon get you a good one."

David murmured appreciation, took the letter from Sneir as if in a trance and slipped it into his jacket pocket. He gathered up the utensils and stumbled down the tunnel.

"So the Tory is trying to get me a job?" David muttered to himself. "And all the time I thought he was sending a secret message."

"You're a good boy!" Sneir shouted down the tunnel. His words echoed and re-echoed along the dark, stone corridor. They seemed to mock David, spelling doom to his hopes of going to Ticonderoga.

6. The Invisible Message

Entering the Phelp's kitchen, David found the family seated for supper, the table board piled with chargers of venison, salmon, spring greens and golden brown biscuits. There were hearty greetings from Matt and Roxy that partially restored David's sagging spirit. Uncle Noah arose instantly and motioned to David to follow him into the study, despite Aunt Lydia's plea to let David have some supper first.

Unhitching his knapsack and canteen, David plopped into a chair and faced Noah sadly. "I couldn't find out anything," he said with a sigh.

Noah squeezed David's knee gently. "I'm sorry. I'm afraid I sent you on a wild goose chase."

"Sneir was friendly enough," David explained, "but he complained that everyone was trying to get him to talk about Ticonderoga. He was in no mood to talk to me about it even though I think he believed my story about being loyal to the king."

"Why do you think he believed you?"

"Because he is trying to get me a good job in New York. He wrote a letter to a friend there."

"Wrote a letter!" Noah exclaimed, rising to his feet. "What did he do with it!"

"Why—he gave it to me to get it to the driver of a New York stage in Hartford. It's just to a friend about a job for me. Here, I'll show it to you." David reached into his jacket pocket.

Noah grabbed the letter, his hands shaking. Taking the letter to a window, he read the address on the envelope, "Robert DeLancy, King's Head Tavern, New York." David watched, puzzled, as Noah broke the seal and extracted a single sheet of paper. He held it close to the window, paused, and turned it over. He came back slowly.

"There's nothing written on the paper," Noah said in a disgusted tone. He showed David a blank piece of paper.

David looked at the blank paper in amazement. "Sneir said he was writing a friend in New York to get me a job there."

Noah shook his head. "This beats me. He hasn't written anything. Wait a minute! I've heard about spies using lemon juice to write with. It's invisible when it dries. I think when you heat it up you can see the writing again. I'll get a candle."

Noah dashed out of the room. David looked again at the blank piece of paper, muttering, "I don't think Sneir could have written with lemon juice. He never had any lemons."

Returning with a lighted candle, Noah grabbed the paper and held it a couple of inches above the flame. David saw hope fade from Noah's eyes as nothing happened to the paper. Tossing the paper to a table, Noah put an arm around David, saying gently, "Let's have supper, Davey."

David followed Noah into the kitchen where Matt and

Roxy looked at David with questioning eyes. Aunt Lydia heaped meat, fish and greens on David's porringer and filled his tankard with milk. He relished the food, despite the disappointment gnawing at his insides. He could see Matt and Roxy squirming with curiosity.

The minute the meal was over and the children excused, Matt dragged David outside into the twilight, trailed by Roxy. Stopping at the well, Matt grabbed David's arm and said, "All right, cousin. Come up with the facts. What's this all about?"

David sat on the stone wall of the well, faced Matt and Roxy, and sighed. "I don't get to go to Ticonderoga. Your father was going to let me go if I could find out from Tory Sneir in Newgate Prison what he saw in Fort Ticonderoga when he was there. But the Tory wouldn't talk. He gave me a letter to send to New York but your father opened it and there was nothing written on the paper."

Roxy looked at David, her eyes wide with surprise. "Is Sneir a crazy man? Who would send a letter with nothing in it?"

"No, he's not crazy." David said. "But you've got a point, Roxy. There's got to be some meaning to that letter."

"Maybe he had two pieces of paper," Matt ventured. "He wrote on one and by mistake put the blank one in the envelope."

"Wait a minute!" David cried. "He did have two pieces of paper. One was crumpled up and thrown aside. He was drying the other over a candle when I arrived. He said it was wet from the dampness in the mine."

"I bet he wrote with some secret ink that had to be dried out to become invisible." Matt said.

"Uncle Noah already thought of that," David said. "Spies are supposed to use lemon juice for ink. It disap-

pears when it dries and reappears when heated. But nothing happened when Noah heated it over a candle."

"What else could he have used?" Roxy asked

"I don't know," David said. "He might have had something in his pockets. All I saw was a bar of soap, a razor, a mirror and a pencil—and sealing wax."

"Ha!" Roxy exclaimed. "The plot thickens. Was the rumpled piece of paper wet?"

"No, I don't think so. Why?"

"Then why would only the other piece of paper—the one in the envelope—be wet from the dampness in the mine?"

David slid to his feet. "I don't know. It doesn't make sense, does it?"

"I know what!" Roxy screamed. "I read a story about a beautiful princess imprisoned in a tower. She wrote a secret message to her prince using her hand mirror to write on. She needed a very smooth surface to—"

"Sneir had a mirror," David interrupted, his interest growing.

"And she placed a wet piece of paper on the mirror. Then she put a dry piece on top of the wet. She wrote on the dry piece and it made an impression through to the wet. When the wet piece dried the writing became invisible."

David looked at Roxy in astonishment. He hugged her and cried, "You smart little monkey! I think you call that a watermark process! Then if we wet Sneir's letter, the message ought to be visible again!"

"You're both nutty as a fruitcake," Matt scoffed.

"Get the letter! Roxy—please," David asked. "And a lantern."

Roxy scampered into the house as David grabbed the handle of the windlass at the well and began cranking feverishly. The bucket came bouncing up, spilling water, just as Roxy returned with the letter and lantern.

David plunged the paper into the cold water as two eager faces and one skeptical face peered intently at the letter.

"I see writing!" Roxy screamed.

She reached in and grabbed the paper. David took it from her gently and laid it flat across his knee.

Shaking with excitement, David held the lamp over the paper and read, "My dear De Lancy: Captain D. urges all haste in sending reinforcements to him at T. He reports fewer than 40 men fit for duty. Your obedient servant, S."

David and Matt looked at each other, mouths open in amazement. Roxy gave a little squeal and ran into the house. She reappeared, hauling her father by the hand.

David, his face aglow in the lantern light, held out his hand with the wet message spread across his palm. Roxy held the lantern close while Uncle Noah peered at it, fingering the words as he read the message.

He turned to David, excitement in his eyes. "That's good news, Davey. You've done us a great service. You'd better get to bed, soon. We've got a long walk tomorrow."

David followed his Uncle and Matt into the house. His mind was filled with soldiers marching with muskets raised and banners flying as they advanced on Fort Ticonderoga.

Roxy trailed behind, her eyes glistening with tears.

7. "He'll Never Make a Soldier"

David drew a deep breath as he stepped through the Phelps' doorway into the early morning sun. "Ticonderoga, here we come!" he whispered in excitement. "The redcoats will sure be surprised!"

It was warm for April 28th and David perspired in his borrowed leather jacket with the fringed sleeves. He would have dispensed with his black felt cocked hat, preferring an old coonskin, but Noah said the cocked hat would provide better protection from rain. And he would not need the warmth of a fur hat.

Uncle Noah, Matthew and Roxy were waiting for him at the well. "Roxy and I are walking you to the river," Matt explained, as Noah let go the bucket and motioned the group forward.

His canvas knapsack felt unusually heavy on his shoulders. But it was only half the size of the pack carried by Noah. Checking the rest of his equipment, he touched his canteen bobbing at his side and his sheathed hunting knife on his right. Reaching back, he fingered the tomahawk strapped to his belt, beneath his pack. He looked down, admiring the gloss on his leather boots, a shine that he knew would be coated with dust within the first mile.

He was missing two items, however, and this bothered him. His uncle carried a musket and a leather cartridge pouch. Neither item had been offered him. He particularly admired the musket Uncle Noah carried. The walnut stock had engraved silver plated on both sides, silver bands at intervals along the length of the long barrel and a brass front sight. But the musket was 5 feet long and David imagined it would be a cumbersome thing to carry in deep woods.

David turned and looked into the sober faces of Matt and Roxy who were trailing behind. He guessed they were unhappy at being left behind. Glancing back at the big house set against the mountain, David felt a certain sadness, too. He guessed he was becoming fond of his adopted home, his lively cousins and kindly Uncle Noah and Aunt Lydia—and in less than a fortnight.

Turning to Uncle Noah, David said, "Why aren't we crossing the river by the toll bridge?"

"Because the toll collector is a gossip," Noah answered, hitching his pack to a more comfortable position. "We must keep our expedition a secret, otherwise the British will get wind of it and be ready for us at Fort Ti. The toll collector would spread the news all around the village."

"But isn't the Simsbury militia going with us?"

"No. The Connecticut Committee of Safety insists that all the militia companies in the Hartford area remain here as a back-up for the drive to oust the British from Boston. We may recruit men only from the distant villages in western Connecticut and Massachusetts."

This surprised David. He wondered how they'd go about enlisting men for the expedition while still keeping it a secret.

Uncle Noah stopped at the river bank and Matt and Roxy caught up. David felt a gentle touch on his arm and looked into cousin Roxy's upturned freckled face. Her green eyes were filling with tears. With a twist of her head and a downward glance, she fumbled at the pocket of David's jacket. Then she darted off toward home like a skittery colt.

David looked at his jacket and found a bouquet of delicate, pale blue hepatica protruding from his pocket. These six-petaled spring flowers were his favorite. "The little rascal," he murmured.

His mood was shattered by a rough grip on his arm. Matt's eager young face pressed toward him. "Get me a British soldier, David."

David was startled. It was as if Matt treated the expedition to Ticonderoga as a bear hunt only they were to bring back British soldiers instead of bear. Well, wasn't this what he wanted—revenge for his father?

A shouted greeting from across the river revealed Uncle Elisha waiting on the opposite bank. Elisha, although a little older than Noah, was thinner and not so tall.

A flat-bottomed scow was tied to a tree at the river bank and Noah and David stepped in cautiously. The weight of their heavy packs made them unsteady. Matt untied the boat and jumped in, sending a series of ripples out into the stream. He grabbed the oars and rowed them across the muddy river with strong rhythmic strokes punctuated by loud grunts.

Elisha reached down and steadied the bow as Noah and David disembarked. Matt backed the boat off and then rested his oars while he turned and raised a hand in a farewell salute. Then turning the boat, he was off for the other shore.

"We'll go by the North Road," Noah explained to Elisha and David. "We're to meet Captain Mott and a couple of his men at the crest of the hill where the North Road meets a trail from Hartford."

Leading the way up the bank, Noah followed a path he said would take them, unobserved, to the North Road. Elisha followed without comment. David chose to bring up the rear so he could set his own pace and observe the sights. Already he had gone beyond familiar territory.

The oak and maple leaves were only half out and provided little shade for a sun that was unusually hot for late April. But, on occasion, the path led through pine groves and David welcomed the cool fragrance of the pines and the soft layer of needles underfoot. He was disappointed when they reached the dusty North Road and the forest gave way to open farmland.

After an hour of plodding on the level, the road started a sharp rise to the western hills. David began to feel the weight of his knapsack.

Noah called a halt at a spring and David knelt down, cradled water in the palms of his hands and drank greedily. He emptied his canteen and refilled it with cool water.

Elisha and Noah rested their muskets against a tree and sat down against the trunk. David decided this was the time to bring up the subject that was bothering him.

"Uncle Noah," David said, "when do I get a musket?"

Noah and Elisha looked at each other, frowning. Noah turned to David and said, "I'm afraid you don't get a musket, Davey. When I agreed you could go I didn't say that you could go as a militiaman carrying a gun."

David drew back as if struck by a musketball. "What's

the point of going if I can't have a gun! I want to have a real part in this expedition. I want to give the British back what they gave us. I want to get even—"

"Whoa, Davey," Noah interrupted, "there's more to winning a battle or capturing a fort than shooting a musket. An army's got to eat, for one thing. Your Uncle Elisha here, for example, is in charge of getting us fed. He isn't complaining."

David picked up a rock and slammed it into a nearby oak. "I bet I'm supposed to chop wood, build cooking fires and that sort of stupid stuff!"

Noah sighed. "That's what we had in mind, Davey. That's why I put the fire starter in your pack and gave you the tomahawk."

"David," Elisha added, "haven't you heard the old saying, 'An army marches on it's stomach'?"

David grunted.

"Even water is vital," Elisha continued. "Just a canteen full of water could save a campaign."

A lot of rot, David thought. He wished he had never come along. He would get a gun somehow. He wasn't going to be cheated out of a shot at the British.

Noah looked at the sun and commented that it was time to move on. He patted David on the shoulder but David twisted away.

It was a steep climb to the crest of the ridge but David vowed he wasn't going to lag behind. He'd show 'em he was as good a soldier as anyone.

Reaching the top, David enjoyed the breeze and the great view east and west. The road west seemed to lose itself in a vast expanse of green forest that stretched to the horizon. Only a few faint traces of smoke here and there indicated habitations.

Looking back east, David found he could still see a few

houses in Simsbury. He located the river and his eyes followed it until he found Uncle Noah's house. He wondered what his cousins were doing now. He would miss them.

"Here they come!" Elisha shouted, pointing down at a trail to the east. "They've got a pack horse with them."

David watched as three men ascended the trail. The third was an old man leading a pack horse. David recognized the first man as Captain Mott, the horseman who had ridden to Simsbury with the message for his uncles.

Noah and Elisha ran down the trail to greet Captain Mott. After an introduction to the other two men, David saw Mott glance in his direction. Here we go again, David thought. I suppose Mott wants to know why I've come along. Well, he'll never get a chance to say I can't keep up.

David wondered how six men and a horse were going to capture Ticonderoga. They'd sure have to recruit a lot of men along the way.

His question was answered when Captain Mott said, "I sent a message to Salisbury a couple of days ago. We should have men waiting for us there tomorrow night."

Noah brought Captain Mott over to where David was sitting on a boulder. David jumped up.

"Captain Mott," Noah said, "I want you to meet the lad who went into Newgate Prison and found out what no one else had been able to discover—what Tory Sneir found out at Ticonderoga."

Captain Mott held out his hand and David grasped it, liking the young officer immediately.

"Your uncle has told me of the Tory's message," Mott said, "and we're delighted to know they need reinforcements at the fort. You're a brave lad as well as clever. We're glad to have you along on the expedition."

David murmured his thanks. It was on the tip of his tongue to ask Mott if he could have a musket but he decided that would be taking unfair advantage of Noah.

Noah suggested they break out some food as the position of the sun indicated noon. David drew out the biscuits and fried chicken legs Aunt Lydia had packed for him. He ate in silence as the men talked of the route they would follow. David felt alone and excluded.

Rising to renew the march, Captain Mott suggested that Noah and Elisha stow their muskets and cartridge pouches under the brown canvas cover on the pack horse. They didn't have uniforms and he didn't want any guns visible that might disclose the purpose of their expedition.

David wished he could add his knapsack to the load on the horse, but he knew better than to propose it. His pack felt as if it were filled with fieldstone.

David took a place in the line of march as Mott motioned them forward. He found himself alongside the old soldier leading the horse. He stared at the soldier, observing his moth-eaten bearskin cap and dirty, stained leather jacket. The man walked with a rolling, bowlegged gait. His face was as tanned and wrinkled as the buckskin of his breeches.

"I'm Dan'l Dreyfes," the old soldier said, extending a gnarled hand.

David grasped the hand, feeling its strength.

"I suppose you wonder how an old geezer like me gets to go on this expedition?" Dreyfes said, anticipating David's curiosity. "Well, it's like this. This expedition needs a gunner if we're going to capture the cannon at Fort Ti. I'm a gunner. I served with Amherst when he took Louisburg in fifty-eight."

"I'm—glad we have you along, sir," David said.

The old soldier chuckled.

Further talk died out as the road climbed one hill after another. David's legs soon wearied at supporting the extra weight of his pack. And the straps chafed his shoulders like hot iron. He welcomed level stretches on the road as a sailor delights in a calm sea following a storm.

David watched the sun sink low in the west with a feeling of relief. They would have to camp soon.

But when Captain Mott called a halt there was no rest for David. Noah gently reminded him that he was responsible for gathering firewood, setting the cooking fires and keeping the firewood replenished.

Unhitching his tomahawk from his belt, David walked wearily along the forest's edge seeking dead wood. His eyes caught a lone hepatica, its blue petals radiant in the last rays of the sun. He picked it, remembering with a smile of pleasure, little Roxy's gift of hepatica. long since wilted in the hot sun. Holding it to catch the sunlight again, he decided to keep it and sketch it in his copy book. Roxy would like that.

As he put the flower carefully in his jacket pocket, he noticed Noah and Elisha watching him. Feeling guilty about idling, he turned back into the woods to renew his search for firewood. Finding a white pine with many dead branches, he began hacking away.

It was getting dark when David concluded that he had chopped enough firewood for the night. Heading for the road with his last armful of wood, the darkening shadows about the campsite reminded him of lurking Indians and he tried to imitate their silent tread. He got within earshot of Noah and Elisha without being heard. As he approached, he saw Noah shake his head as he said to Elisha, "That David—I'm afraid he'll never make a soldier. Imagine a soldier on the march stopping to pick flowers."

David stopped, anger and resentment flushing his face. Just because he enjoyed flowers and beautiful things didn't mean he couldn't be a good soldier. He'd show 'em!

8. Mud, Misery and May Flies

David awakened to the shock of cold rain spattering his face. The early morning sky was a dull gloomy gray and the sound of rain on the dead leaves near his head was a dismal drum beat. He lay under his blankets feeling the dampness seep in and smelling the odor of wet wool.

His shoulders burned from the straps of his pack. He ached all over. Noah's words came back to taunt him. "He'll never make a soldier," Noah had said.

Raising on an elbow, David was surprised to see Noah huddling over a crackling fire that was spitting at the raindrops. Noah looked up and said, "You'd better get up and get your blankets into your knapsack before they get soaked. We should have pitched tents. I've got some coffee going here. And I'll broil a little ham."

The others were stirring now and cursing the weather. Only the horse seemed unmindful of the rain as he ripped mouthfuls of young grass along the side of the road.

Forcing himself into a sitting position, David reached into his pack and pulled out his cloak and boots. With his boots on and his black waterproof cloak covering him, he felt a little better. He found his cocked hat where he had hung it on the branch of a tree, shook it free of water and pressed it tight on his head.

Noah handed him a steaming mug of coffee. Never fond of coffee, particularly black coffee, David found it bitter but, nevertheless, he was grateful for its warmth. A large chunk of crisp broiled ham completed his breakfast.

Subdued by the rain, the men said little more than necessary to break camp. Captain Mott ordered them forward.

David found his usual position next to last, trailed only by Daniel Dreyfes leading the pack horse. "This rain ain't going to last," Dreyfes prophesied. "The wind is shifting." David hoped he was right.

The little army plodded on in gloomy silence, cloaks flapping in the wind and glistening with rain. The road turned to mud as the rain continued and the cloaks soon became splattered with a brown ooze.

David wondered how many more dreary miles to Ticonderoga. He guessed it was at least two hundred. He groaned at the thought of tramping all that distance. Maybe Noah was right. He wasn't cut out to be a soldier.

About midmorning David was cheered by the end of the rain and the appearance of a feeble sun. But his joy was short-lived as the road dipped down into swampy lowlands where insects swarmed about his head and nipped at his exposed face and ears. "May flies," Dreyfes grumbled, cursing the varmints.

The little gnats were a torment. They swirled in clouds around each man's head, nipping at ears, eyes and nose. Even the horse snorted and shook its head.

David brushed the pesky creatures from his eyes and ears and spit them from his mouth. He struck out at them, trying to bat them away. They persisted through the full length of the mile-long swamp. For once he didn't mind the rise in the road that took him to higher ground and freedom from insect territory.

After a rest stop and lunch, David began to feel somewhat better, although his sore shoulders were worse than ever. And when he struggled to his feet to resume the march, his stiff joints rebelled. But after a few yards he found himself back in a shuffling stride that ticked off the miles in a mechanical fashion.

In midafternoon everyone was dismayed when clouds blotted out the sun again and the rain pelted them worse than ever. They found shelter in a barn by the side of the road while Elisha went to the farmhouse seeking hot food.

"It's too bad we can't go to the house and dry out by the fire," Mott said, "but I don't want any farmer plying us with questions. We can't afford to have some Tory carry word of us to the British at Ticonderoga."

David thought that if the British could see this little bedraggled army they'd have a good laugh. He took off his cloak and pack and stretched out on a pile of hay. He was almost asleep when Elisha returned with a kettle of soup.

Dreyfes pushed his long nose over the kettle and pronounced the soup to be Scotch broth. Whatever it was, David accepted a mug of it, welcoming its flavor and warmth.

Captain Mott stuck his head out the barn door and frowned. "It's raining as hard as ever, but we must continue. We're expected in Salisbury tonight."

David groaned. How he'd just like to curl up in the hay and sleep through the storm! He caught Noah's eye on him. Pride made him straighten up and appear eager to go on.

Emerging from the barn, the six sodden soldiers were buffeted by wind-driven rain that had increased in intensity. Lightning flashed and thunder rolled and echoed along the hills. The rain pelted them with stinging force. Even the horse seemed unhappy as he held his head down and snorted.

David staggered along. The rain drove in at the neck of his cloak and trickled in cold rivulets down his spine, chilling him. Water found its way down into his boots. It penetrated his cloak at the shoulders, stinging the sores developing there.

I've had it, he thought. Noah's right. I'll never make a soldier. But he plodded on. There was nothing else to do.

He was reaching the point of exhaustion when Mott shouted that he had sighted a structure ahead. A large saltbox house became visible in the gloom, its great center chimney gushing smoke that was scattered in all directions by the force of the wind. David drew a deep breath of the fragrant wood smoke and found it a tonic, promising warmth, shelter and food.

The men were ushered into the kitchen by a gaunt gray-haired woman who was introduced as Mrs. McVittey and who obviously had been expecting them. Her husband came in with a fresh load of firewood.

David was much too tired to resent the way Mrs. McVittey fussed over him as if he were her child. He relished the stew she gave him and gulped down a pint of warm milk. He didn't resist when she showed him a spare bedroom and ordered him to bed.

9. North Toward Ticonderoga

Beneath a huge patchwork comforter, David slept soundly, unaware of the tramping overhead as Mott's group and the men who had been waiting for them prepared to bed down on the long stretch of canvas-covered hay in the attic. He heard none of the whispered plans discussed with the ten new recruits from Salisbury. Nor was he aware of the starlit sky and new moon as the weather cleared.

He awakened with a warm sun in his eyes and a pleasant, comfortable feeling. Even the normally doleful sound of the mourning dove seemed cheerful. He looked about the room and was delighted to see his clothes, all dried and brushed, laid neatly over a chair.

Quickly dressing and throwing water on his face from a bowl on a washstand, he tracked the delicious aroma of breakfast to the kitchen. Here he found Mrs. McVittey by the fire, stirring porridge in a huge kettle that hung from a crane over the flames. A large spider, with meat in bubbling brown gravy, sat on its three legs over the glowing coals. He detected bread being baked behind the iron door of the brick oven to the right of the huge fireplace.

Mrs. McVittey looked up, brushed strands of gray hair

from her face and peered at David critically. "You didn't brush your hair."

David shrugged his shoulders. He hadn't planned on brushing his hair until he got back from Ticonderoga.

"Here, have some tea," Mrs. McVittey said, " while you're waiting for breakfast." She handed David a mug.

David looked at it, exclaiming, "I thought we weren't drinking tea until the British removed the tax?"

Mrs. McVittey laughed. "Taste it. It's made of young strawberry leaves. We call it 'Liberty Tea'. It's a little bitter but I've put plenty of honey in it."

Strawberry leaves. What a weird idea, David thought. He sipped it carefully. All he could taste was the honey.

"Here, help me set the table," she said, handing David several square boards with their centers hollowed into bowls.

"What are these?" David asked.

Mrs. McVittey looked at him with an expression of astonishment. "Surely you've seen trenchers before?"

David shook his head.

"Land of Goshen, lad, I don't know where you've been. You eat off trenchers. You don't think I'm going to serve a lot of foot soldiers with my china?"

David guessed that was a smart idea but he'd never seen wooden trenchers in Concord or Simsbury. He set out sixteen trenchers around the table board and put a pewter knife and spoon at each place.

There was a tramping of feet on the back stairs and three strangers appeared who he assumed were Salisbury men. David was surprised to see that one with dark hair appeared to be near his own age. The boys eyed each other inquisitively.

Soon the other men appeared, including Noah and

Elisha. Noah came over and said, "Davey, I've talked with Mrs. McVittey. She'll be glad to keep you here until we get back. All her boys have grown up and gone."

David looked at Noah, dumbstruck. Anger and fear combined to color his face. "Uncle Noah! You made a bargain and—"

"Wait a minute, Davey. Hold your horses. I'm not going back on my word. You seemed so beat up last night I thought you'd like to give up this crazy idea of coming with the army."

"No, sir!" David said firmly. "I'm not going to be left behind!"

"All right, Davey," Noah said, squeezing David's shoulder. "You've kept up so far."

David's anger subsided. He sat at the table considering the men as his companions and equals. Having shared with them the hardships of the first two days of march, he felt a part of the expedition for the first time, but he wasn't sure they felt that way about him.

His eyes met those of the dark-haired boy who seemed to be sizing him up. David wondered how the youth had managed to get permission to come along. He soon found out.

Captain Mott ordered all the men outside and David found the dark-haired boy attending two pack horses brought by the Salisbury men. His face was screwed into a frown as he tightened the pack straps. David settled his own pack on his shoulders, noting with satisfaction that some felt pads Mrs. McVittey had given him protected his sore shoulders. He walked over to the youth.

"I'm David Holcomb," he said, "of the Simsbury militia."

The boy's frown changed to a warm smile as he leaned

back against a horse and looked at David. His black eyes were deep-set in an oval well-tanned face. A mass of straight dark hair hung over the collar of his leather shirt. Instead of breeches he wore fringed leather trousers. His leather boots had moccasin bottoms.

"I'm John Tantaquidgeon," he said, grinning, "and I'm drummer for the Salisbury militia."

"How come you have no drum?" David asked.

"It's a sad tale," the boy replied. Turning toward the horses, his face wrinkling in disgust, he added, "It seems this expedition is supposed to be secret, although I don't see how sixteen men and three horses can march along a road without causing a commotion. Anyway, I couldn't bring my drum as it would show we're an army. So the only way they'd let me come with them was to be the horse handler."

David decided he liked this dark-haired boy. "I was allowed to come along—without a gun—provided I build fires and fetch water."

"No fighting with a gun, huh?"

"No."

John laughed. "We'll see about that."

"What do you mean?"

"We'll see. You be patient."

Captain Mott set off at a fast pace, with the others following in two's and three's.

David fell in beside John who led his two horses.

Dreyfes and his horse kept to the rear under Mott's orders to watch for any suspicious strangers who might be following the little band of soldiers.

With cool clear weather David was able to admire the mountain ranges to the west. They were the highest he had ever seen. The road was north through a dense hemlock forest, without any signs of habitation. Yet he was surprised to find an apple tree here and there along the road, ready to burst into bloom. He questioned John about it.

"This is the old Weatogue Indian Trail," John said. "It ran from the Schaghticoke village south of Salisbury to the Stockbridge Indian town in the north. The apple trees just grew by themselves from apple cores thrown aside by the Indians."

David marvelled at this and also at the scenery. Suddenly the road burst from the forest to lush meadow as it ran alongside a broad clear river.

"Housatonnuck River," John said.

David saw a cluster of fat pink flowers on slender green stems bobbing in the breeze. He dashed over and picked one.

"Whippoorwill's Shoe," John announced.

David looked at the delicate pink sack supported by the long thin stem. Turning to John, he said, "I've always called this 'Pink Lady's Slipper'. How come you're calling it 'Whippoorwill's Shoe'?"

John chuckled. "It's all the same thing, isn't it? That's the Indian name for it."

David let the flower slip slowly through his fingers as he looked at John in amazement. "Are you an Indian?"

John laughed. "Don't you have any Indians in Simsbury? Wait a minute! Hold your horses! Simsbury? That's where my ancestors came from!"

"How could that be?"

"In the lodges of the Schaghticoke they tell of the arrival of the Massacohs from Simsbury after the town was burned during King Philip's War. The Massacohs were my family's tribe and I had an ancestor who was the tribe's sachem. The Massacoh village was called, Weatogue—home place."

David's eyes widened. "Your ancestors must have known my ancestors! I was born in Concord in the Massachusetts Colony but my mother came from Simsbury."

"I hope they didn't fight each other," John murmured.

"I'm sure they didn't," David assured him. "My cousin Matthew told me the early settlers of Simsbury lived in peace with the Massacohs. It was the Wampanoags who burned Simsbury during King Philip's War."

David looked at John's pleasant, friendly face and couldn't imagine him with an upraised tomahawk and scalping knife. Curious about John he said, "Do you live on a reservation?"

John snorted. "You'd never catch my father living on a reservation. He doesn't like any one telling him what to do, whether it's a tribal sachem or a village sheriff. We have our own farm and it's way out in the hills—away from everyone."

"Then how did you happen to muster with the Salisbury militia? I wouldn't think your father would like you bossed around by a drill sergeant or company officers?"

"Well, it's this way. I went to school of course. My father insisted on that. And when I told him about King George and all the taxes and things he got so mad he was ready to unsheath his old knife and go stalking the king. I guess I joined the militia so he'd stay at home. I have five younger brothers and sisters."

David smiled, picturing the send-off John's brothers and sisters must have given him when he left with the militia. Of course Matt and Roxy had seen him off but it wasn't quite the same as your own brothers and sisters.

It would be fun having John along. Things were looking brighter. Even his pack felt fairly comfortable now.

The little army came to a halt at a grassy area where a glistening stream tumbled into the river. Noah asked David to gather firewood and build a fire as all the men would be grateful for hot food.

It was difficult for David to find wood in the meadow because of the scarcity of trees. And what he was able to find was soaking wet from yesterday's heavy rain. He hunted in vain for birch or cedar bark as the natural oil in the bark would ignite readily, regardless of how wet it was. As a substitute he selected a piece of swamp maple from his pile of wood and used his hunting knife to shave off small pieces. He shaped the shavings into the form of a miniature tepee with a hollow center.

Taking his round leather tinderbox from his pack, he drew out a piece of iron shaped like a small horseshoe and a flintstone. He stuffed the inside of the mound of shavings with a piece of charred linen cloth from his tinderbox. Then he struck the iron with the flint, sending a shower of sparks against the charred linen. The cloth caught and held a spark, a little ring of fire spreading across the cloth. David blew on it and it burst into flame. But the cloth burned out and the shavings failed to ignite. He threw the flint down in disgust.

John came over and touched his shoulder. "Wait, I'll get you a fire quicker than a groundhog can pop into his burrow."

David sat back on his heels, expecting John to bring some rubbing sticks. To his surprise John returned from the pack horses with a musket cartridge. David watched as John bit off the end of the cartridge paper and poured the powder into the hollow center of the shavings.

"Where'd you get the cartridge?" David asked.

"Never mind," John said, with a furtive glance at the men talking in a group a few feet away. "Just strike some sparks—quick."

David leaned close to the shavings and struck the flint against the iron, sending sparks at the gunpowder. With a whoosh, flame and smoke enveloped the shavings.

"What was that!" Captain Mott exclaimed, running over to the fire.

"I—I just started the fire," David stammered.

"I know that!" Mott thundered, "but only gunpowder could cause a flame like that. Where'd you get the powder?"

David hesitated. John stepped forward, saying boldly, "I used a cartridge from the Salisbury supplies."

Mott grabbed John by the wrist. "Listen here soldier —if that's what you pretend to be. No one in this militia lights fires with cartridges. We save our cartridges for the enemy. Get that straight!"

"Yes, sir," John said, with no show of meekness or emotion.

The captain stalked off.

"Old iron pants," John said with a snort.

10. A Shadow in the Firelight

Noah told David they had crossed the line into the Massachusetts Colony and would be camping for the night outside of Sheffield. The army wouldn't enter that town or Great Barrington as they didn't want to alert the people to their mission. There were some suspected Tories in the area.

The sky was hazy with a threat of rain, so the officers ordered tents erected and several campfires built. David groaned. As chief collector and chopper of firewood, he figured he would spend the whole evening gathering wood. But John offered to help him, for he had already tethered the horses in a little grassy glade and his chores were done.

Captain Mott had selected a small open area in the forest, away from the road, in which to establish camp. It was a pleasant spot and David wished he could prop himself up against a tree, take out his copy book and sketch the scene. The peaked, brown canvas tents were pitched in a circle and already fingers of fog were reaching in from the river to touch the tents. The scene reminded him of the stories his father had read him about Druid ritual sites in ancient England. He could easily imagine the tents as great standing stones and any minute the Druids in their white robes would come gliding into the circle to perform their mysterious dances.

Above the trees to the west the tallest mountain David had ever seen was just catching a glow from the last misty rays of the sun. He wished he and John could come back someday to climb that mountain at sunset.

His reverie was interrupted by a touch of his elbow. It was John. "Listen, if you don't get out into the woods with that little tomahawk of yours and chop some wood, old iron pants is going to lift someone's scalp, and it won't be mine this time."

David sighed and followed John into the strip of forest between the camp and the road. He tried to match John's swinging, silent stride. Finding an abundance of dead-wood within sight of camp, the boys came back loaded. Captain Mott instructed them to build a large fire in the center of the camp for he wanted to have a meeting with the men. Then they should build a couple smaller cooking fires closer to the tents. It was almost dark with no promise of a moon before the fires were built and David and John went to the river and returned with four leather pails of water for cooking.

The boys didn't find the camp food exciting. The Salisbury men had brought along a large supply of salted meat and dried vegetables. Tripods of sticks were erected over the cooking fires from which the men hung black kettles filled with stew. John tasted the stew and made a face, saying he wished they had time to fish in the river or hunt for rabbits or woodchucks for more exciting food.

Captain Mott overheard John's remark and said in a sarcastic tone, "You'd better concentrate on your duties, Tantaquidgeon. See that the horses are properly tethered for the night. And you, Holcomb, get another couple pails of water to have on hand for breakfast."

The boys groaned. John headed for the horses and David grabbed the pails and threaded his way through the dark forest toward the road and the river. Moonlight filtering through the edges of clouds gave him just enough light to find his way.

He reached the road, which ran alongside the river, and stopped, silent, as he thought he heard hoofbeats. Who would be coming along this lonely road in the dark?

Stepping cautiously back into the forest, he waited, his heart beating fast. He held his breath while straining to hear. The river made gurgling sounds, there was an occasional quick rustle in the thickets which he guessed was a night bird or a field mouse. In a distant bog a few last peepers were sending up a faint chorus. But there were no hoofbeats.

He let out his breath and relaxed. Probably he was mistaken or perhaps John had stirred up his horses and some trick in the atmosphere made the noise seem to come from a different location.

Reaching the river, he filled the pails, climbed the bank and stood in the road enjoying the view of the campfires flickering between the trees, sparks rising like fireflies to the dark sky. The silence of the night was suddenly shattered by a deep throaty "whoo whoo whoo whoo whoo" followed by an erie cry that resembled the yelping of a dog and the squalling of a cat. It sent chills up and down David's spine even though he recognized it as the call of the Great Horned Owl. It seemed to come from the spot where the horses were grazing.

David entered the forest and headed for camp, feeling his skin prickling on his scalp. The forest seemed a scary place. He guessed that if he were a cat his hair and tail would be standing straight up.

The owl called again, its last notes particularly shrill

and piercing. David stopped dead, shivering as he saw the dark shape of a man's head pop up in the forest between him and the firelight. The man seemed to look toward the grazing area as if curious about the owl call. He ducked down again.

David set the pails down quietly, and trembled. Someone was spying on the camp! Probably someone who came by horseback!

Sinking to his knees, David strained his eyes to pierce the dark forest and see the stranger again. What could he do? If he shouted to the men in camp the stranger would run away. If he ducked around in a wide circle and into the camp the stranger might be long gone.

He stood up again and saw the dark outlines of the militiamen, huddled in their cloaks and sitting in a circle around the central fire. Captain Mott stood over them. This was the conference Mott had planned—and the stranger was hearing it all! Maybe he would ride to Ticonderoga and warn of their coming!

David's teeth chattered but he knew what he had to do. He fervently wished he could walk as silently as John. Gently brushing branches aside, he cautiously put one foot forward and then another. No sound. So far, so good.

He put another foot forward and accidentally kicked a fallen branch. It rustled dead leaves. David froze. Nothing stirred ahead.

In the stillness David could hear the voices of the militiamen in camp and the gentle rustle of leaves overhead, stirred by a breeze. He took another step and another without making a sound.

Boldly he took several cautious steps. Now what? He must be quite close to the spy. Suppose the spy has a gun? David felt frantically for his tomahawk and found he had left it in camp.

Perhaps he could drive the spy right into camp! He sank to his knees. He'd better crawl now.

David inched forward, his hands and knees seeking spots free of leaves and fallen branches. He strained to see and his ears were tuned for the slightest sound ahead. His heart pounded so hard it hurt. His breath came in short gasps. He felt like a wild animal stalking its prey.

Was that dark shape ahead a fallen tree? He stretched to see. Suddenly the dark shape exploded into the figure of a large man! David sank back on his heels, opened his mouth to shout and was stunned by a smashing blow across his face as the spy crashed into him and fell to the ground. David's lip and nose hurt horribly and he tasted blood.

Angry, hurt and desperate, David cried out and lunged at the spy, grabbing a foot as the stranger struggled to get up. The spy jerked loose, leaving David holding an empty boot. But the spy was thrown off balance and fell again. David pounced on him with a triumphant shout.

A savage blow in the stomach sent David reeling and gasping for breath. He lost his grip and the spy scrambled to his feet and thrashed through the woods toward the road.

David felt sick. He heard what sounded like an Indian war whoop down by the road and a tremendous crashing about him as the militiamen came storming through the woods. He barely recognized Noah who gently guided him back to camp.

In the warm and friendly glow of the fire, David touched his aching upper lip and throbbing nose. Noah pressed a hot cloth over his face which helped relieve the pain.

"Who was it, Davey?" Noah asked, examining David's cut and bruised face.

"I don't know," David said. I thought I heard hoofbeats when I went for water. Then on the way back, I saw someone hiding at the edge of the woods and listening in on your meeting.

"Why didn't you shout for help?"

"I was afraid he'd get away. I was sure he was a spy and might get word to Ticonderoga that we're coming. So I crept in to try to capture him."

Noah put his hands on David's shoulders, looking at him closely. "You've got a lot of courage, Davey. He could have had a pistol or a knife. I got a glimpse of him running. He was a big man."

Noah's praise helped David endure the pain.

David and Noah turned to watch the noisy return of

the militiamen who burst into the firelight dragging the spy. He was a large middle-aged man dressed in expensive tan breeches and a brown frock coat. The men pitched him to the ground by the central fire and gathered in a circle around him.

David looked at the flabby, sullen face of the spy, feeling more curiosity than hatred.

"Tar and feather him!" shouted a Salisbury man. "Send him packing."

Captain Mott prodded the captive with his boot, saying, "This is your last chance to tell who you are and what you were doing here. You heard the demand to tar and feather you."

The spy spit into the fire and refused to speak.

Mott drew aside Noah and Levi Allen, leader of the Salisbury men. David heard Mott whisper, "We can't seem to frighten him with the threat of tar and feathers. What can we do with him? We can't let him go. He probably overheard our plans for Ticonderoga."

"I think I know who he is," the Salisbury captain said. "He looks like a Great Barrington merchant named Ingersoll. He's a real Tory—sells tea secretly, too."

"I have a suggestion," Noah said. "Someone can take Ingersoll, if that's his name, into Sheffield to the Committee of Safety there. I think their headquarters is at Daniel Dewey's Tavern. We can ask the Committee to hold him—at least long enough so he can't beat us to Fort Ti."

"Great idea," Mott said. He immediately ordered two Salisbury men to get the three horses and take the spy between them to Sheffield.

John suddenly appeared at David's side, examined his face, and whistled at the cuts and bruises. "He really clobbered you," John said sympathetically.

Mott, seeing David and John together, came over. Addressing Noah, Mott said, "We owe these boys a great deal. If it hadn't been for them, that spy'd been on his horse and well on his way to alert Ticonderoga."

"Who caught the spy?" Noah asked.

"Oh, didn't you know?" Mott said. "John pounced on him out in the road just as he was about to mount his horse. The men caught up with him before he could break away."

"But if David hadn't pulled one of his boots off," John said, "I wouldn't have caught up with him."

"We sure make a good team!" David said, brightening up.

John turned a sober look on David. "I've got to teach you the cry of the Great Horned Owl before you get into real trouble. The horses were skitterish and I knew someone unfamiliar to them must be prowling about. I gave the owl call. It was my warning to you to be careful. Next time you might get shot!"

David looked at John, his mouth opening in astonishment.

11. The Stream
Becomes a Roaring River

"Sixteen men and three horses," John said with a laugh, looking at the little column as it plodded north toward Ticonderoga. "How can we capture a big fort with such a dinky little army? The British won't even want to waste gunpowder on us."

"At least it's unlikely any Tories or British spies will report us to Fort Ti," David said. "No one but a nut would believe we're an expedition to capture the fort."

John grunted. "Maybe I don't want to carry out my little scheme of getting us muskets for the fight. We'd be better off staying out of it."

"What's your scheme?" David asked eagerly.

John opened his mouth to reply but turned his head at the approach of a tall stranger on horseback. The boys moved up the column, John dragging his packhorse along, eager to listen in on any conversations.

David admired the stranger's fine blue waistcoat, tan breeches and sleek, black cocked hat. His hair was powdered and tied in a long queue at the back. David thought he looked like a wealthy squire accustomed to giving orders.

The stranger reined in his chestnut stallion, bowed to Captain Mott and said, "I'm Colonel John Easton of Pittsfield. Your messenger arrived this morning. I can promise you fifty men and—"

The militiamen interrupted the colonel with a cheer and crowded around him. David looked at John, his eyes shining.

"I don't think all of you should enter the village," Colonel Easton continued. "You're too many to pass off as a hunting party." Addressing Mott, he said, "I suggest you select a half-dozen to come with me to Pittsfield—as guests at my tavern. I'm afraid the rest of your men will have to camp in the woods and keep out of sight."

Mott nodded. "That's wise. But how are you going to recruit fifty men in Pittsfield without creating a stir?"

"Mostly from the Berkshire militia in the neighboring towns," the Colonel said. "Two men here. Three men there. I've men out recruiting them already. And I think we should send someone to Albany for supplies. We can't collect enough food here in Pittsfield for sixty-five men without arousing suspicion."

David and John rested their elbows on the packhorses and looked at each other glumly.

"Guess who gets to sleep in the woods?" John said.

"Us." David said sourly. "The horses, six or eight men and us."

"But that's the end of old iron pants Mott," John whispered.

"What do you mean?" David said, wrinkling his brow.

"This new man's a colonel. He outranks Mott. And even if he didn't, he's got fifty men—that's fifty votes. They'll vote Easton the leader."

"But Mott was commissioned by the Connecticut Committee of Safety to lead this expedition."

"So what, we're in Massachusetts, now."

David shook his head unhappily, remembering Mott's ride into Simsbury and his careful planning of the expedition. But he thrilled at the thought of the little column of men swelled by fifty new militiamen.

Turning to John, David said, "Our little stream of men is turning into a mighty roaring river."

"Where did that come from?" John said. "You sound like my schoolteacher."

"Oh—my father was a schoolmaster," David said quietly. He smiled absentmindedly, his thoughts centered on the expedition. Now they had a chance for success! He wondered what scheme John had for getting muskets.

Suddenly David became aware that eight or nine men were marching off on a side road. He and John were left with Mott, Noah, Elisha, Levi Allen of Salisbury, Dreyfes and the horses.

"Are we all staying at the tavern?" David asked Elisha who was taking some of his personal gear from one of the packhorses.

"Yes and no," Elisha said with a grin. "I'm going to Albany for supplies. The horses are needed for loading in the village. Uh—well, you and John sort of go with the horses. And—well, you bed down in the loft over the carriage shed at the Colonel's tavern."

David's jaw sagged. John's face showed no change.

Dreyfes shuffled over and laughed. "It could be worse, boys. Once with Amherst in fifty-eight I had to sleep in a chicken house—no other shelter from the rain. While I was sleeping one of those durn old hens laid an egg in my hat. Never knew it 'til I put my hat on."

David and John looked at each other and burst out laughing.

Colonel Easton turned his horse and led the little group toward Pittsfield. Topping a rise in the road, the village came into view. David was surprised at the large number of houses and the amount of carriage traffic.

Approaching the village, people greeted Colonel Easton from all sides. The Colonel explained Mott, Noah and Elisha as wholesale merchants from Connecticut and indicated that the horses carried their goods.

Reaching a large tavern with weathered siding and two massive chimneys on each end, David saw what looked like a committee of a dozen men waiting to greet them. Each had a tankard in hand. A huge man wearing an apron stood by a big barrel ready to dole out tankards to Colonel Easton and his guests. David heard Easton tell Mott this was the Pittsfield Committee of Safety waiting to greet them.

John caught up with David and said, "I'm not unhappy we're bedding down in the carriage shed. That tavern is going to be jumping tonight. They'll be sleeping three in a bed and snoring like fifty buzz saws."

"I guess you're right," David said. "I'll help you with the horses. There won't be any firewood for me to fetch tonight."

The boys unhitched the packs from the horses and stored them in a barn. A stable boy led the horses into a shelter.

Noah came out a rear door of the tavern and said, "Wash up at the pump, boys. Then go into the kitchen for some rabbit stew. You might as well eat now before the men come in."

David and John splashed cold pump water over their faces and trooped into the huge kitchen. An enormous log fire burned in the great fieldstone fireplace. A large woman stood by the fire stirring the stew in a big copper kettle which was suspended by a crane over the fire.

"Sit down, boys," she said, grinning at them with a display of broken and missing teeth.

John whispered to David, "How'd she escape the latest witch hunt? I wonder what secret potion she's brewing in that kettle?"

"I don't care what it is," David said. "It smells wonderful."

The woman ladled out huge servings for the boys in large porringers and they dipped into the stew eagerly.

As the boys ate, the men began to tramp into the ordinary room of the tavern, their jovial comments audible to the boys. The whole atmosphere of the expedition had changed with the promise of fifty men from the Berkshire militia.

"And wait 'til my brother joins us!" shouted Levi Allen of the Salisbury militia.

"Who's his brother?" David asked John.

"Ethan Allen. He used to live in Salisbury, too. He bought some land in the Hampshire Grants and moved up there. I've heard tell he's always having fights with men from the York province who claim they own his land. So he organized a big band of men to defend their land. I think they call themselves the Green Mountain Boys."

"Are there many Green Mountain Boys?"

"A couple hundred—oh! oh! There goes another change in command in our expedition. Ethan Allen is a colonel—same as Easton. But he has more men than Easton to vote him in as boss."

David wondered at the fairness of this as the boys finished the stew, gulped down some cider, mumbled thanks and went outside again. It was already dusk and getting rather cool.

"John, let's find a good spot in the hayloft while it's still light," David suggested.

"I'm for it," John replied. "I'm tired enough to sleep already."

The boys picked up their packs and canteens and entered the cavernous carriage shed, admiring the sleek coaches, sleighs and wagons. They climbed a ladder at one side, emerging into the musky, fragrant gloom of the hayloft.

Smoothing the hay level in a corner of the loft, the boys rolled up in their blankets on the hay.

David sighed with contentment. "I wouldn't give two shillings for that tavern tonight. Hot and smelly with tobacco smoke; noisy—whew! They can have it!"

"Me, too." John added.

The boys were quiet for a minute, each wrapped in his own thoughts. David's thoughts turned toward Ticonderoga. Facing John, he said, "What do you think it'll be like, fighting to capture the fort?"

John hesitated and then said, "I think it'll be one of those things where you'll be scared silly while you're fighting, but after it's all over you'll be powerful glad you were there."

"But how do you suppose we'll get into the fort?"

"I guess we'll have to build ladders and climb over the walls."

David stared at the dark rafters of the barn. Fear, for the first time sent shivers through his body. He drew his blanket tighter to his chin.

Of course they'd have to climb the walls of the fort;
They had no cannon to smash the walls down. And all
the time they were raising the ladders and climbing them,
the British would be shooting at them—maybe even
firing cannon!

David pictured the scene and shuddered again.

After an interval David said, "What did you mean
about having a plan for getting us guns?"

John propped himself up on an elbow, looked at David
and said in a low voice, "You know those packs my
horses have been carrying? One pack has several spare
muskets. When we go to capture the fort, old iron pants
is sure to order us to stay back with the horses. We'll
just grab ourselves some muskets and trail along behind.
As soon as the fight starts, they'll be glad enough we're
there with guns."

David gasped, startled by John's plan. He felt con-
fused. He wanted, desperately, to take part in the battle,
but could he take a gun like that against Noah's orders?
Was he so sure he had the courage to stand up against
the guns of the fort?

12. One Colonel Too Many

The march northward had carried the little army across
the border from Massachusetts into Bennington in the
Hampshire Grants. This was Ethan Allen's domain. Here
Allen and his Green Mountain Boys had banded together
to defend their property, granted by the New Hampshire
Colony, against a counterclaim by New Yorkers.

Sitting on their packs, backs against a large sugar
maple, David and John watched with excitement as a
dozen men crossed the Bennington village green. Captain
Mott, Noah, Levi Allen and the officers of the Berkshire
militia waited expectantly for them at the door of Cata-
mount tavern.

John called David's attention to the leader of the
group. "It must be Ethan Allen. He's the only one in
uniform. I understand he designed it himself."

The leader's green coat and buff breeches were gay
in comparison with the drab, informal clothing of his
men. David admired the gold buttons, gold braid and
gold epaulets that glistened in the sun as he walked.

"He looks like a leader," David commented, seeing the
height and strength of the man and the purposeful way
he strode across the green.

Levi Allen stepped down from the tavern doorway and embraced his brother. The Connecticut and Massachusetts militia officers swarmed around Allen's men with much handshaking and backslapping.

"I guess I don't mind if Allen becomes the leader of our expedition," John said. "He's got a rugged bunch of men. And they've all had experience fighting—even if it was only against men from the York province."

Noah broke away from the group and turned toward the boys. "I've got a job for you lads. We need supplies before we head directly for Fort Ti. Take two horses, go out east among the farms and see if you can buy some cornmeal, bacon and whatever staples you can get."

David and John scrambled to their feet. Noah handed David a small leather pouch. "You've got ten shillings in there. Spend it wisely."

Noah hurried off as the boys looked at each other in astonishment. David punched John, exclaiming gleefully, "No fires to build today! No water to fetch!"

"Let's get the horses," John said. "It isn't even noon yet but let's get going before your uncle changes his mind."

The boys sought out Dreyfes who had been placed in charge of the whole packhorse train. Dreyfes grumbled, "I don't know what this army's coming to. Tarnation! Imagine letting children run off with horses and a bag of money!"

David saw John bristle at the word, 'children'. He grabbed John's arm. "Let's get going."

The boys left their knapsacks with Dreyfes, selected two of the better horses, mounted and started of at a trot. David led John out on a road to the east.

"Where're we headed?" John asked.

"I don't know," David tossed back over his shoulder.

"It just feels good to be in a saddle instead of walking. I figure there are more farms to the east wrere the land isn't so hilly."

Outside Bennington village the boys rode side by side, enjoying the countryside. The maples were almost in full leaf. The fields were lush with a new growth of grass. A bluejay flashed across their path with a sharp cry.

David was reminded of John's owl call the night they captured the Tory. "Say, John. You promised to teach me the cry of the Great Horned Owl."

John laughed, threw back his head and emitted six long, low, throaty calls, followed by a piercing shriek that rose and fell in a series of wild calls. The horses snorted nervously.

David opened his mouth wide and shouted a loud screeching imitation. "How was that, John?" he asked proudly.

John looked at David with a blank expression. "I'd say it was a cross between a dying wolf and a lovesick cat."

"Oh, come on," David complained. "It wasn't as bad as that."

"If any owl came in answer to your call, it'd have to be a pretty stupid owl."

"But I'm not calling owls."

"No, but the point is, you make an owl call so other people—maybe your enemies—think it is a real owl. Only your friends know it is you."

"Couldn't we choose a less complicated owl—maybe a screech owl?"

John sighed. "My people use the Great Horned Owl's call because it carries great distances. You can shout your head off yelling 'help' or something like that and it won't carry more than a half mile. But I've been hunting with

my father and heard his owl call twice that distance."

"You win," David said. He threw back his head and tried again.

"Good!" John exclaimed. "Did you see your horse shake his head? When your horse gets skittish you know you're getting close to the real call."

Further attempts at a call were interrupted by the appearance of a farmhouse on their right. David said he would see what they had to sell. John held the horses at the gate while David approached the kitchen door. He was wary of the broken porch rail, decayed floor boards and general appearance of neglect.

In response to his knock, a woman opened the weathered door. She carried a thin, pale baby. Graying hair fell over one eye and her face was wrinkled and worn. Her dress was faded and stained.

"Excuse me," David said. "I'm seeking to buy some food for a—hunting expedition. We need cornmeal, bacon—things like that."

The woman looked at David and her eyes fell on his money pouch. "We have precious little food in this house. My man is a very poor provider. But I could spare you some dried apples."

David wondered what they could do with dried apples. "I don't really think we need dried apples," he said.

The woman sighed.

David saw her disappointment and said, "On second thought, we could make apple tarts."

The woman brightened and turned into her pantry. She came out with a large canvas sack which contained the apples.

David opened his money pouch and gave her a shilling. She turned the coin over in her hand and murmured a quiet "thanks."

David carried the sack out to John and tied it in back of his saddle.

"What did you buy?" John asked.

David pretended not to hear.

John repeated his question.

"Oh, I thought it would be nice to have some dried apples," David said casually.

John looked at David, his eyes widening. "You can't be serious. I can just imagine what the men will say after a hard day's march when you drag out your little old bag of dried apples! She must have given them to you. Surely you didn't buy them."

"I gave her a shilling," David said weakly.

"Next thing I know, you'll be buying ginger cookies," John scolded. "Let me buy the food at the next farmhouse."

John had his chance a minute later as they pulled up in front of a more prosperous-looking farmhouse. John dismounted, took the money pouch from David and strode down a boardwalk to the kitchen door. David reached into the sack of dried apples, looked ruefully at the mass of wrinkled brown fruit and popped a few into his mouth.

Ater a long wait, John returned with a triumphant smile, carrying two large, heavy sacks over his shoulder. He hung one on each side of his saddle, announcing gleefully, "This is more like it. One sack is full of corn meal and the other is jerked venison. And I paid only a shilling for each."

David sheepishly offered John some dried apples, saying, "I guess you're in charge of supplies from now on."

John took a handful of dried apples, remarking, "Do you realize we haven't had anything to eat since breakfast?—and that wasn't much. I think that looks like a tavern ahead at the next crossroads. We've earned the right to lunch at the expedition's expense."

David agreed and the boys urged their horses forward.

The tavern was an unpainted, weathered saltbox with a center chimney. David couldn't read the faded sign. But two horses were tied to a hitching post so he figured there must be at least two customers.

The boys entered the ordinary room and wrinkled their noses at the sour, stale odor of ale and tobacco. A tall, thin, bald man in a leather tunic was wiping the mugs on the counter with a dirty rag.

John whispered to David, "If he's that thin from eating his own food, it can't be much good."

The tavern keeper looked up. "What can I do for you boys?"

"What do you have on the fire ready to eat?" John asked.

"How'd mutton suit you?"

John shrugged his shoulders. David said, "That'd be fine."

David wondered where the other customers were.

The tavern keeper came out with a dented pewter charger heaped with slices of greasy mutton and what appeared to be turnips. He placed the charger on a scarred pine table, set out tin plates and cutlery for the boys and returned to wiping mugs.

David and John found the turnips surprisingly tasty, despite their pale and shriveled condition, but the mutton was tough. John whispered, "You can't tell me this is mutton. It's tough enough to be from a bearded old goat."

The boys were quite hungry, though, and managed to demolish the mutton and turnips in short order. The tavern keeper asked them if they wanted more.

"No, thanks," David replied, "but we're out buying

food for a large hunting party. Do you have any bacon, jerked meat or parched corn for sale?"

The thin man looked at David. "You wouldn't be from Connecticut, would you? Your accent sounds different. By any chance are you with a captain Mott from Hartford?"

Startled, David wasn't sure what to reply. He thought he'd better stall a bit.

"Why do you ask?" he said.

"Well, I have a Connecticut gentleman here—upstairs. He's just ridden in with his servant from Cambridge in Massachusetts. He asked me if I'd seen Captain Mott and his men."

David turned this startling news over in his mind. At the time he had left Concord with Noah, Cambridge was where the Continental Army headquarters was being established. Perhaps headquarters had sent them a message.

"Yes, I'm with Captain Mott," David admitted.

"Good." The thin man replied. "I'll bring the colonel down." He tossed his rag over the counter and mounted the stairs.

"Colonel!" John exclaimed. "What now! Haven't we enough colonels?"

There was a pounding down the stairs. Into the room strode a heavyset, dark haired man in a scarlet uniform.

David gasped. "British—"

The stranger laughed. "I'm Benedict Arnold, Captain of Second Company, Governor's Footguard of Connecticut. We copied this uniform from the British—when we were friendly with them."

David relaxed.

"The tavern keeper called you colonel," John said.

"I am, now," Arnold explained. "I was in Cambridge for the Lexington alarm. The Cambridge Committee of Safety commissioned me a colonel with orders to recruit

400 men to capture Ticonderoga and bring back the cannon to raise the siege of Boston. They told me Captain Mott had left Hartford with men for Ticonderoga. I want to find him. I understand you are with Captain Mott."

"We are," David said. "We're out buying supplies. Captain Mott and Colonel Easton have 60 men right here in Bennington. Ethan Allen is here with some of his Green Mountain Boys."

"Splendid!" the colonel exclaimed. "I'll get my man, go into the village and take charge." With this he sprang up the stairs, two at a time.

"Wow!" John burst out. "Wait 'til Ethan Allen hears this fellow Arnold expects to command the expedition— and with only two votes!"

13. Surprise at Owl's Head Tavern

"We're moving north to Castleton," Noah said, tightening a strap on his saddle. "It will take us two days. And we'll need to carry food as the farms are few and far between."

"Could John and I buy food again?" David asked eargerly.

"That's what I had in mind," Noah said. "You did a good job the other day. I'll stick to the main road with the army. You and John take side roads to find farms we don't. I've arranged with Dreyfes to free up those two horses so you can use them again."

John looked at the sky and shook his head. "We'll need our cloaks. I think it's going to rain."

Noah pulled a worn, linen map from his pack and showed David a small village where the army would spend the night. "Meet us there," he said. "And don't buy any more dried apples."

David winced.

Noah mounted his horse and rode off.

"I wish we could see the meeting between Arnold and Allen," John said. "Where'd Allen go, anyway?"

"He went north to recruit his Green Mountain Boys for the expedition. He's going to meet us at Hand's Cove on Lake Champlain. It's opposite Ticonderoga. Arnold went chasing after him."

The boys swung into the saddle and trotted east again. The sky was a dull gray and David felt a dampness in the breeze. The tops of the hills were shrouded in mist.

David offered John a handful of dried apples from a pocket bulging with them.

John accepted the fruit with an expression of disgust. "Have we got to eat the whole sack of this stuff by ourselves? If the seeds were still in, we'd be planting a trail of apple trees all the way to Ticonderoga and back."

Turning north at a crossroads, the boys rode on, enjoying the scenery and speculating on what life might be like in this area. They passed several farms without remembering their mission. The sight of a farm with a pen of hogs jolted them to the fact that they weren't out for a joy ride. Bacon and ham were much wanted commodities.

By agreement, now John was the buyer of foodstuff. He trotted down the lane and returned a few minutes later with a side of bacon and two large hams. "That took most of our money," he said. "We only have enough left for a couple sacks of meal."

"And a meal for us at the Owl's Head Tavern," David added. "I saw on Noah's map that there's a tavern on this road a few miles north."

"Great!" John said. "Because I'm hungry already and I just felt a drop of rain."

"I did, too," David said. "Let's get going."

They dug their heels into their mounts as the rain descended. But it was a warm rain and their cocked hats and cloaks fended off most of it.

The Owl's Head Tavern came into view at a crossroads and they welcomed the sight of the sturdy inn with its colorful sign and smoke pouring from huge chimneys at each end. John examined the owl on the sign and commented that the artist sure wasn't much of a naturalist. His owl seemed to be a cross between a screech owl and a great horned owl.

Taking their horses to the stables at the rear, the boys entered the kitchen door, shaking water from their hats and cloaks. David noticed sacks of meal stacked up by the door.

The proprietor greeted them and David was glad to see he was fat. His food must be good.

"How much for a couple sacks of meal?" John said.

"I'm sorry, boys," the man replied. "They're not for sale. I've already sold them to the British."

"The British!" David and John said in unison. "What are they doing here!"

"Sh!" the proprietor replied, glancing nervously toward the door to the taproom. "There are two British soldiers in there now. They've bought the meal to take to Fort Ti."

"Let's get out of here!" John hissed, turning toward the back door.

"Wait!" David commanded. "What are the British doing here?"

The proprietor motioned the boys to follow him into a corner of the kitchen away from the taproom door. "Here's the story, boys. It's really funny. These two soldiers, one a sergeant and the other a private, are from Fort Ti. They left the fort over a month ago with a wagon, and they've been out buying supplies.

"I get it!" David whispered. "They don't know there's a war on!"

"Right," the man said with a grin, "and we don't tell 'em, because if they knew we were at war with 'em, they'd just take the supplies without paying for 'em."

John grabbed the man's arm, his black eyes shining.

"Let's capture them!"

"Oh no you don't!" the proprietor said. "At least not until they've spent all their money."

David got a sudden idea. He was reminded of Noah's wish to find out about the condition of Ticonderoga and Tory Sneir's message about the fort needing reinforcements.

"I'm going to talk to those soldiers," he stated.

"Are you crazy!?" John exclaimed. "You might let slip about our expedition."

"Be careful," the proprietor cautioned, "I want to get paid for those sacks of meal."

David drew a deep breath and stepped into the taproom. The sight of the red British uniforms made him tremble. The two soldiers lounged at a pine table smoking white clay pipes with long stems. The one with sergeant's stripes was about 30 years old, and the private, about 18. They didn't look up when David entered.

"Excuse me, sir," David said, addressing the sergeant. "The tavern keeper says you have bought those sacks of meal by the kitchen door. My uncle sent me to buy a couple sacks. He's going on a hunting trip. By any chance could you spare a couple?"

The sergeant blew smoke toward the ceiling, rested his pipe on the table and looked at David. "Listen, lad. Those are the King's sacks. I'm taking them to Fort Ticonderoga."

"You're from Fort Ti!" David exclaimed, feigning surprise. "What's it like there?"

The sergeant turned to the private. "He wants to know what it's like at the fort."

The private laughed.

"I'll tell you what it *isn't* like, lad," the sergeant said. "It isn't comfortable. The fort's a bloody mess and there isn't enough food!"

"And we need more men," the private added.

"That we do," the sergeant confirmed.

David had difficulty controlling his excitement. His lower lip began to quiver. Forcing a steady voice, he said slowly, "If you need men why don't you just tell the generals at Montreal or New York to send you some?"

The sergeant laughed, his ruddy face glowing. "I can see you don't know the ways of the army. As soon as the snow melted we sent a man to Montreal to ask for 100 more men."

"Did you get them?" David said eagerly—a little too eagerly, he thought. He'd have to watch it.

"No, not yet," the sergeant replied.

"But they should be there now," the private added. "Remember? The messenger returned just before we left. He said the reinforcements would be at the fort in three weeks. We've been gone over a month."

"So we have," the sergeant agreed. "And the more men the more food they'll need." He sighed and picked up his pipe. "I guess we'll have to head back in a couple of days."

David's excitement was tempered by the bad news that reinforcements probably had arrived at Ticonderoga.

"I'm sorry about the cornmeal," the sergeant said. "As you see, we have a lot of mouths to feed."

"Oh, that's all right," David said, walking toward the door. "We'll try somewhere else."

Entering the kitchen, David grabbed John by the shoulder. Seeing the proprietor busy at his ledger books, he whispered to John, "We've got to get going—fast!"

The boys excused themselves, hurried outdoors, unhitched their horses, and galloped off toward the village where they were to meet Noah and the rest of the men.

# 14. A Brave Offer

The shower ended and the late afternoon sun broke through the clouds as the boys reached the Bull Tavern at the little village on the road to Castleton. Water still dripped from their cloaks and David felt wet at his neck and inside his boots.

The village green was sprinkled with the brown canvas tents of the army. But the shouts and laughter coming from the meeting house indicated that most of the men had gone there to avoid the rain. David wondered why they hadn't gone into the tavern. He had his answer from Dreyfes standing at the tavern door.

"Your Uncle Noah is in the tavern," shouted Dreyfes. "The officers are having a meeting in here."

David bounced off his horse and ran up the path to the tavern.

"You can't come in here," Dreyfes protested. "The "The officers aren't to be disturbed."

"Let me in," David said. "I have news for them."

"It'd better be good," Dreyfes retorted, "or you'll be in trouble."

David pushed through the doorway and plunged into the tavern. The room was heavy with tobacco smoke and pungent with the odor of cider and rum. A fire burned fitfully in a huge fireplace.

Captain Mott was explaining to the officers clustered around a large table that they were to meet Allen and his men May 8th at Hand's Cove on Lake Champlain, opposite Ticonderoga.

Noah looked up, saw David and frowned. "We're busy, Davey," he said. "You can report your purchases later."

"I want to report something else," David said, approaching the assembled officers. "I've just been talking to British soldiers from the fort and—"

"You've what!" Captain Mott exploded.

"John and I met two soldiers at the Owl's Head Tavern. They're out buying supplies for the fort."

"You didn't let them know about our expedition?" Mott demanded.

"No, sir. They've been away from the fort for a month and don't even know about Lexington and Concord. The farmers won't tell them because the soldiers would take their food without paying for it."

"Incredible!" An officer exclaimed.

"You talked to them?" Noah asked, his brow wrinkled in surprise.

"Yes. And I found out that Ticonderoga has received reinforcements from Montreal."

The officers looked at David in astonished silence. The only sound was the crackling of the fire.

"That's the end of our expedition," an officer said, tossing his pipe to the table in disgust.

"How many fresh soldiers did they get?" Colonel Easton asked David.

"I don't know," David answered. "They sent a messenger to Montreal asking for a hundred. The messenger returned over a month ago saying reinforcements would come in three weeks."

"Let's turn around and go home," one officer said sadly. "A hundred men inside that fort could defend it against 500. With Allen and his men we've barely two hundred."

"I wish we could find out how many men they've got now," Mott said, staring into the fire. "Sometimes you ask for twice as many men as you need, hoping you'll get

half as much. I wish we had someone in there spying for us."

The officers lapsed into silence again, brooding on the bad turn of events.

Finally Noah cleared his throat and said quietly, "I'll go up there and spy on the fort."

All heads turned toward Noah. No one spoke. David

looked at Noah with astonishment and pride.

"It would be a very dangerous thing—to spy on the fort," said Israel Dickinson of Pittsfield. "Spies who get caught get hanged."

There was further silence. It appeared to David that the men were giving Noah a chance to change his mind and withdraw his offer. David didn't believe he would.

Suddenly it occurred to David that maybe they would let him go with Noah! What a great experience that would be to get inside the fort posing as Tories. How his father would have liked a chance at that!

"I'll go too!" David blurted out.

Someone laughed. Captain Mott silenced him.

"No, Davey," Noah said. "You're not going."

"Wait a minute," Mott said. "Noah, you'll be a lot safer if the boy goes along. I don't know what excuse you'll give for entering the fort, but if you have David along you'll look less suspicious. Normally you wouldn't expect a spy to bring along a member of his family."

"Can the boy be trusted to hold his tongue?" Colonel Easton asked.

"Indeed he can," Mott replied. "Noah tells me he did a fine job of getting information for us from a Tory in Newgate Prison. And you've just heard from David how he got the two British soldiers to tell him about reinforcements."

"All right, Davey," Noah said. "I don't like it, but you can go."

David gave a whoop and dashed out to tell John. Dreyfes, who had been listening at the door, shook his head and remarked sadly, "Durn fool rabbits headin' straight for a den of foxes."

15. A Den of Tories

Noah said he guessed they must be approaching Skenesborough by the number of smoke plumes ahead. David thought a settlement would be a welcome diversion after the endless forest but he wasn't sure he wanted to pass through this town.

"Why are we going through Skenesborough?" David asked. "I understand it's a den of Tories."

Noah laughed. "That's exactly why we are going there, Davey. In the first place we'd create suspicion if we avoided Skenesborough because it's the shortest and most natural route to Fort Ti. Secondly, it will give us a chance to practice at being Tories. After all, we've got to behave as Tories when we get into the fort."

David accepted this idea with some uneasiness. Although he had made out he was a Tory with Sneir in Newgate Prison, it would be a lot different in a whole village of Tories.

"Were you ever in a play in school?" Noah asked.

"Well—no, not exactly, but I was an angel in a church pageant."

"Hardly training for a Tory," Noah said, laughing.

"But being a Tory is just like acting out a part in a play. Just remember, the performance will last all the time we're in Ticonderoga. You've got to think and act the part of a youth who loves George III and hates all the Liberty Boys and their wild doings."

David groaned. "That'll sure be out of character for me. Couldn't you be the Tory and let me be your wayward son who has taken to running wild with the Liberty Boys?"

Noah chuckled. "We might get away with it, but it'd be a lot safer having you a Tory, too. I don't think you'll find it difficult. Apparently you were very convincing with Sneir."

David wasn't so sure about that or anything else.

"How is it they're all Tories here?" David asked, observing, nervously, that they were approaching a few small log cabins.

"It all started after the French and Indian War. A British army officer, Colonel Philip Skene, who was stationed at Ticonderoga, bought up scores of land grants given his soldiers by the Crown at the end of the war. He accumulated 50,000 acres of land. Then he set out to establish a little kingdom there, with himself as lord of the manor."

"But why does that make him a Tory?"

"Because he has imported slaves, for one thing. And he rents out farmland to poor people who can barely make anything more than the high rent he charges. He supports the Crown because he knows if we defeat the King we won't let him oppress his people this way."

"But I'd think his people would be rebels."

"Probably many are—at heart. But they'd be secret about it. Some would pretend to be Tories just to keep in good favor with the Colonel. The trouble is, we don't know who are which, so we've got to assume all are Tories."

A turn of the road revealed a wide, shimmering ribbon of water extending north, past the settlement. "That's the head of Lake Champlain." Noah explained. "It widens up by Fort Ti and runs north over a hundred miles—almost to Canada."

David thrilled at seeing the great waterway his father had described as the Indian highway leading from Canada down to the American frontier. Many an Indian war party, some led by Frenchmen, had skimmed silently down this lake in bark canoes to ravage the settlements. A few miles north, Fort Ticonderoga stood on a bluff guarding the junction where the Indians could connect with Lake George and paddle even further south.

Two long buildings, one of stone and the other of logs, squatted in the sun along a creek in an ugly setting of rotting tree stumps.

The steady thumping of waterwheels and piles of saw-dust told David one was a sawmill. He guessed the other to be a grist mill.

A row of unpainted clapboard houses was strung along the waterfront. Set apart from the houses, as if in contempt, was a huge stone mansion with massive chimneys that scattered woodsmoke over the smaller homes. Stone stables suggested that the owner enjoyed fine horses. It was apparent to David that the mansion belonged to Colonel Skene.

The fields surrounding the village were freshly ploughed. David observed Negroes hard at work harrowing the brown soil. It looks like a wealthy community, David thought, but he guessed the only one getting rich was Colonel Skene.

"Let's go into the store," Noah said, pointing out a

wooden building by a wharf on the lake. "We could use supplies. And it will give us a chance to play at being Tories."

David followed Noah onto the long porch of the low one-story building. He tensed as Noah opened the door, revealing several people inside.

The store had a heady odor of dried herbs and spice cookies. Animal traps decorated the walls and a collection of boots and shoes hung from the rafters. A customer in soiled work clothes ran his fingers through seed in a large hogshead by the counter. He complained to the shopkeeper that the bean seeds were moldy.

The thin, balding storekeeper leaned over the counter and snarled, "If you don't like the seed, try another store."

The customer went away grumbling. David guessed there wasn't another store for thirty miles. You either took what the store had or went without.

Noah asked the storekeeper if he had any fresh meat.

The man looked at Noah with cold, gray eyes, saying, "Are you a stranger in these parts?"

Two men who had been examining a plow in the corner stood up and came forward, listening for Noah's reply.

"I'm from down Pittsfield way," Noah said. "I've received a message that my sister is very ill up in the Hampshire Grants. My boy and I are on our way to visit her."

"I don't know anyone in Pittsfield," the storekeeper said, "but I know Ingersoll in Great Barrington. I trade with him."

David froze at the name of Ingersoll, the Tory. The storekeeper surely was a Tory if he did business with Ingersoll. This looked like a test.

Noah looked the storekeeper in the eyes and said, calmly, "I know Ingersoll. We get along just fine."

The storekeeper's face seemed to relax. He said, "I thought you might be one of those rebels and I was prepared to throw you out."

Noah laughed. "I wouldn't do business with a rebel. I hope they all hang."

The two men went back to looking at the plow and the storekeeper said he would fetch some venison hanging out back.

David let out his breath and relaxed. Noah had passed the test.

The door burst open and David observed with interest the entrance of a very attractive girl with an expensive gray bonnet and cape. Her oval face was set off by black ringlets. She had a pert little nose. David noticed the haughty tilt of her chin. He thought she was about eighteen.

"Where's Mr. Jones?" she asked, looking at David. "And who are you?"

David swallowed and said, "If Mr. Jones is the storekeeper, he's out back. And I'm David—Phelps." He had almost said "Holcomb." He must remember he is supposed to be Noah's son.

The girl drummed her fingers on the counter. "I wonder where that man is!" She let out an exasperated sigh.

"He just went to cut us some venison," David said. "I'm sure he'll be back soon."

"What a bother!" she exclaimed. "If he doesn't get me that ribbon I won't have it in time for the ball at the fort!"

The mention of the fort sent shivers through David. He saw that Noah was leaning against the counter, enjoying the scene.

Here's my chance, David thought, to pry a little information from the girl. He said, "You're lucky to be so close to the fort. You must have a whole regiment of beaus there."

"Humph!" she pouted.

David drew a deep breath, "I understand there are scores of new soldiers at the fort. That'll make the ball more interesting."

"A lot you know about it," she snapped. "The only new one I've seen is Lieutenant Feltham—and he's old enough to be my father. He's such an old tyrant he won't let any of the new men out of the fort."

David caught Noah's eye. Should he go any further? He was thinking how to frame the next question when the storekeeper returned with the venison. The storekeeper returned with the venison. The storekeeper saw the girl and bowed slightly. "I'm sorry, Miss Skene," he said, "the ribbon—"

"Oh, drat!" she said and stormed out of the store.

Noah paid for the venison and bought some dried vegetables. He motioned to David to leave.

As they got outside Noah said, "So that was Miss Skene. Probably the Colonel's daughter. You sure picked a Tory princess to talk to. The way you looked at her I'm not sure I'd trust you to keep your senses in her presence."

David didn't reply. He was bewildered. Somehow he'd never figured on Tories being girls, too.

16. Campfire Strategy

David gathered wood for the campfire with a rapidly beating heart. As soon as he and Noah settled down by the fire he would demand the right to a gun if their spying trip were successful.

A cool, clear twilight and a cheerful fire should have made a pleasant evening but David was uneasy. It was not just the showdown he was going to have with Noah. It was also the uncomfortable knowledge that Fort Ticonderoga was only a couple miles away through the forest.

Noah was busy cutting the carrots and venison into a stew. The fire was going well and the tripod of sticks in place. David had filled the leather bucket from nearby Ticonderoga Creek. There really wasn't anything else needed but David fussed around pushing sticks into the fire aimlessly.

What if he made a mess of things in the fort tomorrow? Suppose the British find out he is a spy? Do they still torture spies to make them talk? What if they make him tell about the expedition?

Noah hung the little stew pot from the tripod so the flames licked at the sooty bottom. He pulled a blanket from his pack and sat down with a sigh.

"Well, Davey," Noah said, peering at David intently,

"here we are, two miles from the enemy and calmly cooking our supper. How do you feel?"

David didn't want to admit to feeling frightened. He said, "I suppose the British will be no harder to fool than the Tories in Skenesborough."

"It depends on how we play it," Noah mused. "We've got to be very casual. We'll make believe we just dropped in so I can get a shave before going across the lake to see my sister. We can look around but we can't ask too many questions"

"But how can we prove we're Tories?" David asked. "Tories don't have have any passes or badges or uniforms or anything."

"That makes it all the easier," Noah said, stirring the bubbling stew with a bent spoon. "We just make believe we're loyal to King George and hate Sam Adams and all the rebel hotheads in Boston. If we just speak like Tories we'll have no trouble."

David didn't think that would be so easy. He had never met a Tory until he talked with Sneir in Newgate Prison. He wasn't sure he knew how Tories talked.

"Get your mug," Noah said, "the stew is ready."

David held out his battered pewter mug while Noah spooned stew into it. It had a wonderful smell. He leaned back against his knapsack and dipped his spoon into the stew eagerly. The firelight sent shadows dancing against the trees. An owl hooted in the distance and he wondered if John were at the meeting place with Ethan Allen across the lake at Hand's Cove.

Finishing the stew, David knew he must confront Noah about the musket. He just couldn't come all this way to Ticonderoga and not have a real part in the fight. For one thing, he owed it to his father.

He coughed to clear his throat. His hands tightened

on his canteen. "Uncle Noah," he said, "if I do all right at the fort tomorrow—ah—I think I ought to be allowed to have a musket."

Noah stopped scrubbing the stew pot with oak leaves and looked into the fire. "Davey, you know the agreement was that you could come along—but without a gun. That's final."

David kicked a log into the fire, sending a stream of sparks skyward. Resentment set his hands shaking. Angrily he burst out, "What more do I have to do to prove I'm a good soldier?! I—helped capture a Tory! I did well at Skenesborough—you said so!"

Noah set the stew pot down and wiped his hands on the tail of his hunting shirt. David waited impatiently.

Finally Noah turned to face David and said, "I have two reasons for not wanting—"

"And one of them is I'm too young!" David interrupted, his tone bitter.

"Not necessarily," Noah said softly. "Too immature but, perhaps, not too young."

"Too immature! How do you figure that out?"

"Davey—"

David interrupted again. "Why do you call me 'Davey'? It sounds like a child's nickname."

"It's not a child's name—David. It's a family nickname. Your father used it. Many families have names they just use for each other."

"Well, I don't like it," David said stubbornly.

"All right, David," Noah said. "Now let's get on with the discussion. First, I have an obligation to the memory of your father and mother to give you protection and guidance."

David shrugged his shoulders and stared into the fire.

"Second, you've been under a severe strain with the

death of your father. You've developed a fierce hatred of the British."

"Is there anything wrong with that?" David questioned.

"Yes and no. You are harboring a deep anger. If you can control your anger you can make it work for you. If you let it control you, you're licked."

David hadn't realized Noah was aware of how much he wanted revenge against the British. But he didn't feel like listening to a lecture.

"I don't see what my anger has to do with my right to carry a gun," David said.

"Anyone going into battle with anger like yours is going to be blinded by it. Your judgment would be impaired. You could get yourself killed doing some foolhardy thing."

David was about to snap back when he realized that would be a sign of his anger. He thought about what Noah had said and his anger at Noah simmered down a little. After a long interval of silence, he said, "Is that really final? What if I show I can control my anger right in the middle of all the British soldiers in the fort tomorrow? Will you reconsider?"

Noah rested his hand gently on David's knee. "Fair enough. We'll talk about it again after we leave the fort. Now let's get some sleep. We have a hard day ahead of us tomorrow."

They rolled up in their blankets and Noah seemed to go to sleep almost immediately. But David couldn't. His mind kept returning to Ticonderoga, no matter how many times he tried to count stars to induce sleep. The fire died down to a few red coals, the night birds stopped their calling and the dew collected on the woolly hairs of his blanket before sleep finally stilled his restless tossing.

17. The Guns of Ticonderoga

Noah emerged from the forest and faced Fort Ticonderoga with feet apart in a defiant stance. Across a half-mile of light green meadow, the fort stood out like the cold, stone castle of an evil baron seeking to dominate the countryside.

Following Noah's footsteps, David stepped into the sunlight and enjoyed the warmth of the morning sun. He looked at Noah, admiring the strength and courage of his uncle. He noted the strong shoulders that carried such a large pack with ease. And he was proud of the contempt with which Noah faced the fort.

Raising his eyes to the fort, David chilled at the sight of rows of black menacing cannon that seemed to point right at him. Fear and anger blended as he saw the crosses of St. Andrew and St. George, the hated British flag, flying smartly in the cool breeze that whipped across Lake Champlain.

Noah turned to David. "It's still only midmorning but we'd better eat lunch now. We can't count on getting any victuals in the fort."

David grunted. For the moment he didn't trust his voice. He knew that entering the fort as a spy would be a fearsome thing, but he hadn't been prepared for the sight of all those terrible cannon. He wondered if Noah and he were already under observation by the British and perhaps some of the cannon had been turned to aim at them.

Unhitching his pack and bedroll, he pulled off his hat and let the breeze whip his thick blond hair. He loosened his leather belt, letting his tomahawk drop to the ground. Sliding his canteen strap from his shoulder, he lay the canteen gently on the grass, admiring the painted design on it.

"I'm a bit worried about that canteen, David," Noah said. "With the coiled rattlesnake and the 'Don't tread on me,' it's too obviously a military canteen. The British may be suspicious of it—and us."

"Since you won't let me have my father's gun—or any gun—at least I should have his canteen," David said, the old resentment beginning to smolder.

"All right, David," Noah said with a sigh. Rumpling David's hair he continued, "You win. Keep the canteen. Now let's rehearse our plan."

As he sliced bread with his hunting knife and cut a chunk of cheese in half, Noah said, "Don't forget our story. We are on our way to visit my sister who is ill in Shoreham, across the lake in the Hampshire Grants. We are stopping at the fort so I can get a fresh shave and spruce up at the regimental barbershop."

"But won't they think it strange that you'd enter the fort just for a shave?"

"No, not at all. There's no nearby town. Everyone passing through this area goes to the fort for supplies, haircuts—everything. Except they won't let you in now unless you're a Tory."

David shuddered, fearful of his ability to act the part of a Tory.

Noah continued. "We'll keep our eyes open, count the

guns and I'll see if I can find out how many reinforcements have arrived. You snoop around and see what you can uncover. With the aid of kind Providence, we'll gather enough information to make it easier to capture the fort tomorrow. Those cannon must be brought to Boston to drive the British out."

David took a chunk of the bread offered him, wrapped it around a piece of cheese and tried to chew it. His mouth was so dry he couldn't swallow. He pulled the plug from his canteen and took a long drink.

Noah strapped his pack on again and motioned to David to do the same. Together they strode through the fields. David kept his head down. He felt better if he didn't look at the fort.

At a log bridge over a creek they joined a road leading to the fort. David stole a glimpse of the fort close ahead, towering over them like some fairy-tale castle. Only this was real. His knees felt curiously weak.

He tried to keep his mind off the fort by watching a red-winged blackbird's graceful swoop across the meadow. He wished he could fly away like the bird but he kept dragging his feet forward.

Now he could hear voices from the fort. It was impossible to ignore the fact that it was there. Looking up he caught the glint of the sun on the steel bayonet of the guard standing by the wicket gate. He shrank, seeing the scarlet coat and white breeches. Memories came flooding back of scarlet lines on the road to Lexington, the awful shooting and the men carrying his father back to the house.

The sentry pointed his firelock at Noah and shouted, "State your name—and business at the fort!"

"Noah Phelps and son, David, from down below Skenesborough, loyal to the Crown. I'd like to get a shave and spruce up before passing on to visit a relative across the lake."

The sentry looked them over carefully while David felt as if he might explode with suspense. Finally the soldier motioned them through the gate with a sweep of his hand.

In silence they entered a cold, dark tunnel leading to the central parade ground inside the fort. The tunnel seemed to David like the muzzle of a giant cannon. Their boots echoed along the cobblestones like the slow measured beat of a funeral procession.

"Keep your chin up, David," Noah whispered. "All you need to do is count the cannon. I'll try to find out the condition of the fort and how many men are stationed here."

They burst into sunlight, finding themselves in the center square of the fort, flanked by two levels of stone and wooden buildings containing barracks, storerooms, bakery, workshops and other facilities. Stairways led to the parapets and cannon.

David felt as exposed as the time he went swimming, bare, in the Sandy River and was carried by the current right down to the middle of the church picnic. Several soldiers in red and white turned to stare at them and David wondered if, somehow, they could tell they weren't loyal to the Crown.

Spotting the regimental barbershop, Noah squeezed David's arm and said in a low voice, "Just wander around a bit. I'll fifind you when I'm through." He strode out of the square leaving David with a feeling of utter loneliness.

David slipped off his pack and bedroll, setting them against the wall by a stairway. Trying to be as inconspicuous as possible, he leaned against the wall and surveyed the interior of the fort, his heart beating rather fast.

He was eager to mount the stairs to the parapet and count the cannon but he thought he'd better not do that so soon as it might arouse suspicion. Noah had said for him to wander about. He would just have to play the part of a boy visiting the big fort for the first time.

Hoping that no one would question his casual sight-seeing, he mustered his courage and began a tour around the inside of the fort. He hoped he wouldn't meet up with a British soldier as he wasn't eager to get into any conversations that might trip him up. There were no soldiers in the square at present but he could hear a number of voices coming from what looked like soldier's barracks on the east side.

David forced himself to walk slowly by the barracks, trying all the time to look nonchalant. Peering in the windows he could see a number of bunks and soldiers lounging about. Some lay on the bunks, some seemed to be playing a game with cards and a few were mopping up the stone floor. Glowing fireplaces at both ends provided heat.

Strolling further around the square he discovered the bakery by its delightful aroma. A man emerged in dirty overalls from a nearby shed and David thought the shed must be a storehouse.

As he approached the west side of the square he was startled to see a young child dart out of a doorway and race back in as a woman's voice called out shrilly. He walked slowly by the doorway. This seemed to be quarters for the families of soldiers. He hadn't expected that! He had pictured soldiers drilling, cannon being cleaned and polished, intermittent drum beats to duty, and soldiers pacing back and forth saluting each other and the British flag. This was more like a little village.

Encouraged by the peaceful atmosphere of the fort, David decided it was time to perform his duty and take an inventory of the cannon and howitzers. Head down, he bounced up the stairs, his canteen slapping his side. At the top he collided with a British soldier about to descend. Shocked by the impact and the sight of a scarlet uniform so close, he drew back against the railing. Prepared to hate the soldier, he was startled to look into a pair of sparkling brown eyes and the pleasant face of a youth about his own age.

With a proud toss of his head the young soldier announced, "I'm Peter Kennett, fifer, His Majesty's 26th Regiment of Foot."

"You're—a soldier?" David asked, taken back at seeing someone so young in a British uniform.

"At your service," Peter replied, snapping to attention. "Can I assist you in any way?"

To hide his amazement, David forced a smile, saying, "Yes, if you don't mind. I'm David—Phelps. This is my first visit to Ticonderoga. I'd like to see the view from the parapet. Would you point out the sights?"

"Glad to oblige," Peter replied, motioning David to precede him onto the parapet. "Only I hope Lieutenant Feltham doesn't see me. He's in a fierce passion most of the time. David barely heard him, gloating at the ease with which he had maneuvered an inspection of the cannon. Reaching the upper platform he drew a breath at the beauty of the lush fields, forest, lake and distant mountains. Then his eyes lowered to the parapet and the ring of ugly black cannon pointing out the apertures.

He saw that the fort was shaped like a giant star so that the cannon could fire at all angles, with no blind spots. Quickly he counted 36 cannon in one point of the star. Since there were five points to the star that made

180 cannon. What the American army couldn't do with these cannon against the British in Boston! They could drive them right into the sea!

Suddenly David got a bold inspiration. He bet Colonel Allen, Captain Mott and the men could use a detailed drawing of the inside of the fort! With a map they'd make no mistakes about the location of the barracks, the powder storage room and other important areas.

Turning to Peter, he said, "The view from up here is wonderful. I have a little talent for sketching. Do you mind if I sketch the view?"

Peter laughed. "I should say not. That fiend, Feltham, has me lugging wood every afternoon from the woodpile to the fireplaces and cook stoves. Take all the time you need. Someone else will have to carry wood today."

Delighted with his good luck, David dashed down the stairs and pulled his copy book and pencils from his knapsack. He returned, found a seat on the stairs and began his sketching.

18. Disaster!

Fort Ticonderoga grew rapidly in David's copy book as his talented fingers sketched every detail.

The sun was pleasantly warm and a breeze brought the fragrance of May from field and forest. The only unpleasant note was the British flag flapping overhead.

Peter straddled the wall, tapping his feet against the stone to the beat of a lively tune he whistled. David wondered if Peter might be dreaming of home in England. The warm spring weather encouraged thoughts of other days and boyhood adventures.

David hurriedly sketched in clouds, sky, forest, fields and lake. After all, he had told Peter he wanted to sketch the view. A burly sergeant mounted the stairs, stared at

David, glanced at his copy book and strode off.

"What's it like, living in the colonies?" Peter asked, his face taking on an expression of sadness.

David put down his pad, thought a moment and said, "I suppose it's just like England. You go to school during the cold weather and work on the crops the rest of the time. Except my father was a schoolmaster and I never seemed to be free of schooling."

"You said your father *was* a schoolmaster. What does he do now?"

David's face clouded. "My father is dead. He died last month—in an accident. My mother died when I was born, so I've come to live with my uncle, the man who brought me here."

Suddenly David panicked, perspiration breaking out on his forehead. He had just told Peter that Noah was his uncle! The plan was for them to appear as father and son!

Peter looked at David closely. He slid off the wall and held out his hand, which David shook. "That makes us even," Peter said. "My father was a grenadier. He died of smallpox in Montreal last summer. Instead of returning to England—my mother is dead, too—I asked to stay on with the regiment."

David flashed Peter a sympathetic smile, but his thoughts were elsewhere. What if that crabby lieutenant hears Noah say he came to the fort with his son and Peter tells Feltham that Noah is his uncle?

"What's your uncle's home like?" Peter asked wistfully.

David put down his pencil. "I've only lived there a couple of weeks, but it's great. The house faces a long ridge of mountains and at the back, there's a river with marvelous fishing."

"It must be wonderful to live in a house like that," Peter murmured, his eyes moistening. Then he looked at David's sketch, exclaiming, "I thought you were drawing the scenery from the fort? Your sketch is mostly of the fort."

Hastily closing his pad, David answered, "I'm really rotten at sketching landscapes. I'm better at buildings, so I concentrated on the fort."

David held his breath, waiting to see if Peter had any suspicions. Peter's face revealed nothing.

"We have a bakery here, you know," Peter said, bouncing down from the wall. "Maybe we can get a few doughnuts."

David was anything but hungry, but he quickly gathered his things together to follow Peter, relieved to put his sketchbook out of sight in his pocket.

Peter led the way at a fast pace. David kept his eyes down hoping not to be noticed. Rounding the corner of the tool shed, David found himself confronted by a red-coated lieutenant whose sleek black hair streaked with gray, beady black eyes and snarling mouth reminded him of an angry raccoon. Peter whispered, "It's Feltham!"

The officer grabbed David by the shoulders and demanded to see the sketch he had been drawing.

"What—sketch?" David stammered.

Feltham snatched the copy book protruding from David's jacket pocket. He opened it and sucked in air through his front teeth.

"Why did you draw the picture of the fort?" he demanded.

David looked helplessly at Peter whose face expressed bewilderment. Drawing a deep breath, he faced the lieutenant and replied, "I was struck by the handsome view of the lake and mountains and tried to sketch the scene.

I'm—well—I'm not very good at landscapes, so I ended up giving more attention to the fort in the foreground."

"A likely story!" Feltham snarled. His fierce eyes fell upon David's canteen. "And where did you get that canteen?"

David's heart pounded. He hesitated, groping for a sensible answer. "A trapper gave it to me down in Skenesborough."

"I've seen that rattlesnake design on rebel militia canteens around Boston. When were you last in Boston?"

"I've never been to Boston," David lied. "I've lived all my life around Skenesborough."

David held his breath and restrained his trembling as the officer looked him up and down.

Turning toward the east barracks, Feltham shouted, "Corporal of the Guard! On the double!"

David shrank against the toolshed in dismay as a red-coated corporal emerged from the barracks and trotted toward them. His musket was extended, from which was attached a long vicious bayonet.

"Lock the boy up!" commanded Feltham. "We'll have a Court of Inquiry tomorrow!"

David gasped as he was prodded by the bayonet. He heard Peter's protests silenced by Feltham as the guard nudged him across the parade ground. He was forced down a short flight of stairs and along an alley to a heavy wooden door. A tiny square opening, with iron bars, served as a window.

The corporal opened the door and shoved David into the damp, sour-smelling darkness. The door was slammed shut. David heard the rattle of a key in the lock.

Shivering in the foul darkness, David stretched out a hand and found a bunk with a straw mattress. He slid down on it and used his canteen for a pillow.

All the tragedy, frustration, anger and disappointments of the last few weeks churned inside David. He drove his fist into the mattress and his anger brought tears. Tarnation! Had he ruined Noah's spying mission? Would Noah be imprisoned, too? If they didn't report to Colonel Allen, would Allen call off the attack, thinking the British knew of his plans?

19. David's Revenge

David lay on the rough mattress and stared at the moist stone ceiling. He could see about the room now that his eyes had become accustomed to the darkness. He twisted and turned in his fury and frustration, blaming himself for his stupidity in openly sketching the fort. He blasted Feltham for catching him.

Suddenly there was a hiss at the tiny window in the door and a voice called softly, "Davey!"

David sprang from the bed and his heart leaped as he saw Noah's face peering in between the bars. "I'm awfully sorry," David apologized.

"Never mind," Noah said. "I heard the story from your friend, Peter. Apparently the lieutenant doesn't know—yet—that I came with you. As soon as he finds out he'll throw me in there with you."

"Get out of the fort as quick as you can!" David pleaded.

Noah's eyes narrowed. "You're a brave lad, Davey. For the sake of the mission I've got to go. How many cannon?"

"One hundred eighty."

"Good boy, Davey! The south wall looks easy to breach and there's just a handful of new soldiers. I heard that much of their powder got wet in a storm last winter!"

David felt a thrill of excitement pass through him.

Noah thrust his hand through the window and David grasped is. "Take care, Davey," he whispered. "You'll be safe in there when we attack tomorrow. We'll get you out."

Withdrawing his hand, Noah disappeared. David slipped back to the bunk, cheered by the knowledge that all was not lost. And he didn't mind that Noah had started calling him "Davey" again.

But it wasn't long before the dismal atmosphere of the dank room, and the cold facts of his own stupidity and imprisonment returned to dishumor him. And he was hungry. He longed fervently to be back in Concord, with his father alive, and the terrible firing only a nightmare.

Night came but David was hardly aware of its arrival. He stared into the darkness, tortured by the past and fearful of the future.

A rattle of a lock and a flash of light sent him scrambling to his feet. The door squeaked open and he looked into the lamplight at the pinched face of a red-coated British soldier who said, not unkindly, "Captain Delaplace wants to see you."

"Who's Captain Delaplace?" David blurted.

"The commandant of the fort. Follow me."

As in a trance, David grabbed his canteen and stumbled after the soldier. They climbed the stairs to the parade ground, the soldier's lamp casting weird shadows that danced along the stone walls of the fort. The soldier led David up the steps in front of the west barracks to a door at the head of the stairs.

The soldier knocked on the door and a muffled voice ordered them inside. When the door was opened, David was startled to see a portly British officer with a fleshy red face seated behind a huge pine desk, his back to a fire. The gold trappings on his splendid scarlet uniform flashed in the light from the flames. Surveying the room, David's eyes came to rest on a figure sitting on a bench. His eyes widened as he saw it was Peter. Peter smiled in recognition.

David watched as Captain Delaplace examined him from his hair to his boots. David stood rigid with anxiety as the Captain's eyes fixed on his canteen—and then passed on.

Finally Delaplace said, "You're lucky you made a friend of Private Kennett. He came to me pleading for your release, asserting you aren't a spy for the rebels."

David flashed Peter a grateful smile and lied boldly, "I'm loyal to the King, sir. I just like to draw every chance I get. I meant no harm."

Delaplace leaned forward with a severe expression. "Who is this man you came with? I met him in the barbershop and he told me he came to the fort with his son. Private Kennett say's he's your uncle."

David's heart jumped but he had prepared for this question. "I am an orphan, sir. I live with my uncle who came with me to the fort. He—well, he has no sons of his own, so he thinks of me as his son."

Watching Delaplace's face, David hoped to see the frown disappear. Instead, Delaplace thundered, "Uncle—father—whatever he is, what kind of a man is he to abandon you in the fort without a protest and slink off like a sneaking Indian!"

David felt the blood drain from his face. Desperately he strained for a sensible reply. Grasping at half-truths he said, "I'm afraid you have misjudged my uncle, sir. He came to the jail—and chewed me out for being so stupid as to draw pictures of the fort. He said he couldn't wait to argue it out with the lieutenant because his sister was dying in Shoreham. He said he'd get me released on the way back."

The captain pursed his lips and turned to Peter. "Do you believe him, Private Kennett?"

"Oh yes, sir," Peter replied quickly. "I saw his uncle leave in a great hurry. It must have been because of his sister's illness."

"All right, Kennett. I'll release this youth in your custody, but I'll issue orders to forbid his leaving the fort until I can talk with his uncle. You can take him to your barracks. There must be an empty bunk."

David released his breath with a quiet sigh. He clasped Peter's hand, his eyes expressing thanks. Peter saluted the Captain who returned the salute with a smile. David bowed. The boys marched out happily and descended the stairs to the cool, starlit parade ground.

Peter led David across to the east barracks. Opening the door slowly he whispered, "Everyone will be asleep. Don't make much noise. Sergeant Ramsey's a light sleeper and when awakened is right surly. His bunk is the lower one to the left of the door. Your bunk is opposite him on the right. Mine is way back in the far corner."

Pressing a slab of greasy ham into David's hand Peter whispered, "You must be hungry. Take this." Then with a friendly smile, Peter retreated into the shadows.

David sniffed the ham in delight and shook his head in disbelief. Here he was about to bunk down with twenty or more British soldiers. And he had just been befriended by one of the finest boys he had ever met— a Britisher. He wondered what John or Noah or Captain Mott would think if they could see him now!

Dying fires at each end of the barracks cast sufficient light to enable David to find the vacant bunk. He set the ham down and unhitched his canteen, hanging it on a peg by his bunk. With a start of surprise he found his pack, bedroll and tomahawk in the corner by his bunk. Peter must have found them on the parade ground where he had left them.

He slid into the bunk, pulled off his boots and drew up a blanket. The room smelled of wood smoke and stale tobacco. There was an amazing assortment of snores. But it was so much better than the jail. He found the slab of ham and chewed it happily.

Too stirred up to sleep, his eyes roamed about the barracks, counting twenty bunks. In the feeble, flickering light from the fires he was able to pick out a soldier in almost every bunk. Red uniform coats and white breeches hung from pegs at the rear wall.

Then his eyes strayed to the front wall and all the past returned with a jolt. Twenty murderous British muskets stood upright in racks, each with a leather cartridge pouch hanging alongside. These muskets were the deadly Brown Bess of the British foot soldier and at the end of each barrel a long savage bayonet stuck out as sharp as a sword. Anger flared up inside him and flushed his face. His heart began to pound. He wanted to strike out at the British. There must be something he could do!

He would tear the guns apart! At least he'd rip out the flints so they wouldn't fire!

Holding his breath, he carefully lowered his stocking feet to the floor. He looked at the sleeping soldiers and stood immobile in the same spot for a full minute to see if anyone was awake. There was no movement or challenge from any of the soldiers. Peter must be asleep by now, too.

He shivered a little and then took two steps toward the muskets. He looked back. Still no challenge. One step more and he reached the first musket to the left of the door. The fires were dying fast and it was difficult to see.

With trembling fingers he explored the cocking mechanism of the first musket, seeking the flint. He groped for it, found it, but couldn't work it loose. He gave a desperate tug and the musket slid into the next one with a clatter. He froze into a statue.

"What's that?" a voice murmured from the first bunk.

David pressed against the wall in panic, trying to flatten himself into the smallest shape possible. He hoped there would be no sudden flare-up of the fire. Then he remembered. Peter had warned him that Sergeant Ramsey, in the first bunk, was a light sleeper.

Scarcely breathing, David clung to the wall for several anxious minutes, fearful the sergeant would fully awaken. All the soldiers remained quiet, however, except for their snoring.

Afraid to attempt a second effort to remove the flints, he tip-toed silently back to his bunk. It was difficult to see. The fires were only glowing coals now. Stooping down to get into the bunk, his head hit his canteen. The canteen! Water! That was it!

David slid the canteen strap over his head, pulled the plug with his teeth and quietly tiptoed back to the wall. This time he approached the leather cartridge pouches, hanging by their straps between the muskets. With tense fingers he opened the cover of the first pouch and explored inside. He fingered the double row of cartridges—small wads of paper, each enclosing its precious load of powder and a musket ball. These balls would be fired at Americans tomorrow—if the powder remained dry!

With a quick glance at the bunks to assure that all the soldiers were sleeping, David tilted his canteen, pour-

ing water over the cartridges. Another glance at the
soldiers. No one stirred.

Elated, David moved down the line of cartridge
pouches, wetting the cartridges. His canteen held just
enough.

He tiptoed back to his bunk and climbed in, breathing
heavily, sweat moistening his brow. Then fear gripped
him as he heard with horror, the drip, drip of water leak-
ing through the bottom seams of the cartridge pouches
and splashing on the stone floor.

Ramsey stirred. David dug his fingers into the sides of his bunk in dismay and waited breathlessly. Ramsey grunted, "Raining again."

David relaxed with a long sigh as the pouches stopped dripping. The barracks darkened as the glowing coals died out and turned to ash.

Suddenly the door was thrust open and someone entered the room, walking quietly. David held every muscle taut as the stranger disappeared into the shadows. What was this all about?

There was a rustle at the back of the barracks and a whisper. "Scott! Wake up! You've got the 12 to 4:00 guard duty." A groan was followed by the noise of a soldier struggling out of bed. The stranger returned to the door and disappeared.

Soon Scott plodded down the aisle, visible to David only as a dark shape. David heard him take a musket from the rack. There was a pause and a slight rustle of clothing. That must be the soldier sliding the strap of the cartridge pouch over his head. David held his breath. Would the soldier find the pouch wet? The door opened and Scott went out.

For the second time David relaxed. Then it dawned on him that Scott would be on guard duty when Allen and the men attacked. And his powder would be wet and wouldn't fire!

David was so excited by this that he couldn't get to sleep. He wished his father could know what he had done—and with his father's canteen, too!

20. Attack!

As the night slowly deepened and the quarter moon set, exhaustion frayed the edges of David's excitement. He finally fell asleep, one lonely rebel in a barracks full of British.

While David slept in the dark and silent fort, the hidden American camp across the lake at Hand's Cove was exploding with activity. The men were excited by Captain Phelps' report that Ticonderoga had been reinforced by only a handful of men. Allen's Green Mountain Boys were still arriving with hunting guns and a fierce resolve to beat the British and capture the fort.

The American camp had no fires. The men moved about as best they could in the dark forest bordering Lake Champlain. Muskets were checked, cartridge pouches filled, belts tightened and knives sheathed. The men glanced nervously at the great shadowy mass across the lake, feeling the ominous presence of Fort Ticonderoga.

All day long squads of men had secretly scoured the lake shore for boats. Colonel Allen looked at the results and shook his head. Two old scows, that's all. Only enough to transport eighty men—half his force.

Colonel Arnold paced restlessly along the shore of the misty lake. Stumbling on an exposed root, he cursed the darkness, the root and the Green Mountain Boys. His anger surfaced as he remembered the whispers and titters of Allen's men, in particular, as they cast their votes against Arnold as commander. And he had presented orders from Cambridge naming him as commander! Wasn't he head of the 2nd Company, Connecticut Footguard? He alone had the proper military training for such an expedition. They told him after the vote that he was to have associate or joint command or something vague like that, and he knew he had to accept this, for first of all, he was a soldier. But it was obvious that Allen now intended to make all the decisions. Arnold stopped pacing and gloomily sank down against a tree. He sat there staring into the darkness at nothing in particular until they called him to the boats.

Most of the Connecticut and Massachusetts men were assigned to the first crossing of the lake. Colonel Easton had them well prepared. The men squatted in the bushes along the shore, packs adjusted, muskets in hand and muscles tensed, ready to spring into the boats when the command was given.

Noah passed the word along the line of men for John Tantaquidgeon to join him in the cluster of officers gathered around Colonel Allen. It was several minutes before John found his way to Noah in the darkness.

"John," Noah said. "You and David have been friends. I'm going to ask you to do David—and me—a favor."

"I'd like the chance to do it," John said. He had been worried ever since Noah reported that David had been locked up in the jail at the fort.

"As you know, David's in the jail," Noah said, "and we're all going to be too busy when we get inside the fort to do anything about him right away. That's where you come in."

"How is that?" John asked, puzzled by the request.

Noah grasped John's arm. "I want you to tag along at the end of the column. As soon as you're in the fort, go to the jail and find David. Try to get him out. If you can't, stand guard at the jail until we have time to come."

"Do I get a gun?"

Noah hesitated. "Yes, you'll have to have a gun. But you have these orders. You're not to go chasing the British. You're to find David."

"Yes, sir!"

John hastened to find the pack horses and the extra muskets. He located them by smell. Quickly securing a musket and cartridge pouch, he returned to the lake just as the command was given to shove off. He leaped into the stern of the nearest scow, its occupants grudgingly making room for him.

Sitting with his musket across his knees, John watched with awe as two heavily laden scows pushed off silently from the dark shore. A score of men sitting along the sides of each scow, paddled quietly with whatever means available. Some had paddles, some used oars as paddles and others used any flat board that could be found.

There was no sign of dawn as yet, but the night was bright with stars. The whole scene seemed spooky to John as the other boat disappeared into patches of mist rising from the lake and reappeared again.

Colonel Easton, Captain Mott and Noah knelt in the bow of John's boat peering into the darkness. They were so rigid John thought they looked like figureheads on a schooner.

The soldiers sat silently in the bottom of the boat. There was only an occasional grunt from the men at the paddles. John thought it amazing that a boat carrying forty men could be so quiet. There was a faint splash from the paddles now and then, a gurgle of water, a muffled exclamation or two—that was all.

John imagined everyone had thoughts similar to his. If they were discovered, a cannon would fire a shell to light up the lake and then the other cannon would let them have it. He had heard the British had the lake divided into zones, with a cannon aimed at each zone, That way they couldn't miss. The night suddenly seemed cold and he shuddered.

The dark line of the western shore finally loomed close at hand. John was glad there was only a faint trace of dawn. He understood that between the fringe of trees at the waterfront and the fort was nothing but open fields- on purpose, he thought, so the gunners in the fort could see anyone sneaking up on them.

Both boats touched shore together and the men in the bows scrambled out. John leaped out into a foot of water and waded quickly to the protection of the alder bushes along the shore. Allen's voice quietly directed them through the bushes to the edge of the field. The boats slid back into the lake for another trip.

Struggling through the bushes, John hoped the sounds wouldn't carry up the hill to the fort. At the edge of the field Allen whispered, "Form two columns. I'll lead one, Colonel Arnold will lead the other. We've got to have a narrow formation to get through the gate."

"Aren't we going to wait for the boats to bring the others?" someone whispered anxiously.

"We can't wait," Allen said sharply. "Look at the sky. Dawn's coming."

John looked at the black shape of the fort with misgivings. He could see the dark line of the parapet broken at regular intervals. That's where the cannon thrust out their black ugly snouts. He shouldered his musket and got into line near the rear.

"Forward, men!" Allen ordered.

"Crouch!" Arnold commanded, bending over.

Stooping low, the two columns trudged up the field toward Fort Ticonderoga. John followed the man ahead of him, seeing only the dark ground and the man's boots. For the first time his feet felt cold and wet from the leap into the lake. The chill traveled up his spine and he shivered.

There wasn't a sound from the marching men except the rustle of grass and heavy breathing. Like John, all had been hunters at one time or another and knew how to walk silently. Crows squawked in the distance and there was an occasional flutter of wings as birds were flushed from the fields by the marching men.

The two columns crawled up the hill like two long segmented caterpillars. All the men were in dark hunting shirts or homespun except for Allen and Arnold. Allen, wearing his green uniform with gold epaulets, was conspicuous at the head of one column and Arnold, in scarlet, stood out at the head of the other.

John felt the column slow down as the dark mass of the fort loomed ahead. Its high stone walls seemed impregnable. He saw the row of cannon and surpressed another shiver.

It seemed to John as if everyone were holding his breath as the columns crept up the last few yards. When would they be seen? The suspense was unbearable.

Suddenly there was a shout. The columns wavered. John saw a sentry aim his musket directly at Colonel Allen. It failed to fire!

"Into the fort!" Allen shouted, running forward with

musket raised. Arnold raced by his side. Both chased the sentry through the wicket gate.

John joined in a great shout as the men followed, storming through the gate with the force of a stampede. They roared into the tunnel like the clatter of a stagecoach on cobblestones. Bursting into the parade ground they fanned out, shouting Indian war whoops. "Come on out and fight, you lousy lobsterbacks!" someone shouted.

21. Victory!

Sudden, massive shouting jolted David awake. His skin tingled with excitement as he realized the attack had begun. "To arms! The rebels are upon us!" bellowed a voice in panic from a nearby bunk.

Sergeant Ramsey scrambled from his bunk yelling to the men to turn out. In the faint light David watched gleefully as the British soldiers stumbled about in their underwear, bumping each other as they sought their uniforms. Ramsey bolted the door, cursed, and shouted, "Forget your clothes! Grab your muskets!"

David shrank down in the bunk and held his breath as Ramsey snatched a musket from the wall, using the butt to break the small panes of glass at the top of the door. He tossed muskets and cartridge pouches to his men.

Raising up on an elbow, David looked out a window and thrilled at the sight of the Americans roistering about the parade ground. He saw Allen race up the stairway to Captain Delaplace's quarters. A startled Lieutenant Feltham appeared from his room below the Captain's, breeches in hand. He was swallowed up in a horde of howling militiamen.

Ramsey grabbed a cartridge from a pouch. About to bite the end off he let out a howl, "How'd the cartridges get wet!" A soldier threw a handful of cartridges to the floor with a cry of disgust.

"Try 'em anyway!" the sergeant yelled as he bit the end off a soggy cartridge and poured a little powder into the primer pan of his musket. He dumped the rest down

133

the barrel and used his rod to ram the wadded musket ball down on top of the powder.

David gasped as Ramsey pointed his musket through the broken glass at Allen as the colonel stood pounding on Delaplace's door. Ramsey squeezed the trigger. The hammer clicked. There was no flash.

With a violent curse, Ramsey hurled the musket against the wall and turned quickly, his eyes scouring the barracks. He was a big man with a great chest and a stomach that had popped two buttons off his underwear.

The sergeant's eyes found David. His great hairy arms reached down into the bunk and grabbed David by the collar. David clawed frantically for a hold on a bunk post. He missed and found himself dragged out onto the floor with a thud. He scrambled to his feet.

"Who are you!" Ramsey bellowed as the soldiers gathered around.

David stood up straight. "Private David Holcomb of the Simsbury Militia!" The soldiers stared at him with stupefied expressions. He caught a glimpse of Peter and winced at the accusing look on Peter's face.

"You're nothing but a rabble-rousing Yankee spy." Ramsey thundered. "And I'm going to run you through with my bayonet!"

David darted around the giant soldier, reached the door and shouted for help through the broken glass. Ramsey grabbed a musket and thrust the bayonet at David. David dodged, his heart racing.

A glance in panic through a window told David no one had heard his call. But he thought he saw John. Throwing back his head, he gave the cry of the Great Horned Owl, its penetrating high notes startling the British.

Ramsey hesitated, the owl call seemed to have thrown

him off balance. Then he lowered his head and charged at David, bayonet pointed at his stomach. David lurched to the right, gasping for breath.

"Let the lad be!" a soldier shouted as he tried to restrain the sergeant by grabbing his right arm. Ramsey broke the hold.

Boxed into a corner, panting, David watched, entranced, as Peter climbed up on a top bunk. As Ramsey crouched for another charge, Peter threw himself onto Ramsey's back, arms around his neck. Ramsey staggered but came on, carrying Peter with him.

There was a crash of shattered glass as a musket poked in from outside.

"Drop that gun!" a deep voice shouted through the window.

Ramsey froze, his face screwed up in rage and frustration. Peter slid off his back. Ramsey slowly relaxed his grip on the musket and it clattered to the floor.

More glass broke as more musket barrels poked through the windows. "Open the door!" someone commanded.

No one moved. David walked to the door and threw the bolt, his hands trembling.

John burst through the doorway followed by Noah, Captain Mott and several Connecticut militiamen. John hugged David and cried, "Am I glad I taught you the owl call!"

Captain Mott looked at the British soldiers. "They're all armed, but no one fired a shot at us!"

"I'll tell you why," Ramsey snarled. Pointing to David, he said, "That young rabble-rouser put water in our cartridge pouches. Our guns wouldn't fire."

Astonished faces turned to David, who blushed.

"How'd you get in here?" Noah asked.

David grinned. "I was let out of jail and quartered here. I used my father's canteen to pour water into the cartridge pouches during the night."

"That's why the sentry's musket failed to fire!" Captain Mott exclaimed.

Noah put both hands on David's shoulders. "You're a brave lad, David—and clever. You saved a lot of lives today."

"And nearly lost his," John remarked soberly. "You should have seen that big sergeant chasing David with a bayonet."

David turned to John. "Was that you—the stern voice that ordered the sergeant to drop his musket?"

"How'd you like my deep voice," John said, chuckling. "I made out like I was six feet tall."

"It sure scared Ramsey."

Ramsey snorted.

"Get your clothes on!" Captain Mott said to the British. "I want all of you outside."

The British dressed silently. David approached Peter who was buttoning his jacket, a gloomy expression on his face.

"Thanks, Peter, for helping stop Ramsey," David said, touching Peter's shoulder.

Peter looked up. "I trusted you—and all the time you were a spy."

"I only did what anyone would do for his country," David said, stung by Peter's animosity.

"But I thought we were friends. I got you out of jail. You just made friends with me to help your rotten spying."

David opened his mouth to protest but Peter pushed David aside and went outside. David followed, his spirits dampened.

All the British soldiers were herded, under guard, into a corner of the parade ground, except for the officers, Feltham and Delaplace and the women and children. Colonel Arnold insisted they be allowed in their rooms under guard.

The sun was up now. David joined John and watched with amusement as the Green Mountain Boys frolicked around the fort. A group found a supply of eight inch cannon balls and had a contest to see who could toss a cannon ball the farthest.

Suddenly there was a shattering roar as a cannon was fired from the upper parapet. The astonished soldiers looked toward the south bastion to see Dreyfes beside a smoking howitzer. He danced around the cannon waving his bearskin cap.

"Get down from that cannon, you old fool!" Allen shouted, his face tight with rage.

Turning to the soldiers, Allen said, "That's enough

tomfoolery. You've had your fun. Fall in!"

The soldiers gathered reluctantly in formation across the southern side of the parade ground. David and John lined up with the Connecticut militia.

Looking across the parade ground, David saw Peter, hands in pockets and shoulders hunched forward, shoved by the guards into the mass of dejected British prisoners.

"What will happen to the prisoners?" David asked Captain Mott who stood with Noah in front of the group.

"They'll be marched to Hartford," the Captain replied. "Probably put in Newgate Prison in your town."

David gasped. Peter imprisoned in that damp, old stinking mine!

Colonel Allen called for attention. Facing the men he was a commanding figure in his green uniform, face flushed with victory and intense burning eyes. He held in his arms the British flag that had flown over the fort.

"Major Brown!" Allen called. "Front and center!"

A young officer from the Pittsfield militia stepped forward and saluted.

"Ride like you've never ridden before!" Allen commanded. "Take this flag to the Continental Congress in Philadelphia and tell them our soldiers behaved with such relentless fury, that they so terrified the King's troops, they durst not fire on us."

The men whooped and hollered as Major Brown strode off with the flag in his arms.

Colonel Arnold, erect and proud in his scarlet uniform, and carrying a musket, walked over to Allen and whispered something. Allen nodded.

"Private Holcomb, front and center!" Allen snapped.

David stood stunned. Someone gave him a friendly push from behind. He stumbled forward, his canteen bobbing, and then marched smartly to Allen and saluted.

Allen returned the salute, his eyes boring into David's. "Holcomb, I'm told you saved my life. At the entrance to the fort the sentry pointed his musket at me and it failed to fire. I understand it didn't fire because you poured water from your canteen into the British cartridge pouches."

David murmured a "Yes, sir."

"Well, Holcomb, we don't have any medals to award yet. We're a new army. Perhaps you can suggest an award."

Allen looked at Arnold who had moved to his side, holding the musket up straight. Arnold smiled at David. There was complete silence from all the men.

David looked at the musket in Arnold's hands. Then he glanced at Peter slumped disconsolately against the wall in the group of British prisoners.

"Sir," David said. "I'd appreciate having a British soldier, Peter Kennett, released in my custody. He was largely responsible for my success in the fort."

Allen and Arnold looked at David as if they hadn't heard correctly. Arnold moved the gun toward David as if David hadn't understood, then withdrew it. Allen opened his mouth as if to protest but Arnold touched his arm.

Across the parade ground Peter Kennett stood up, disbelief on his face.

Turning to Noah, David said, "Could Peter come to Simsbury and live with us?"

Noah stepped forward with surprise on his face and then smiled. "You've earned it, David. Aunt Lydia and I will welcome Peter into our household."

Peter came racing across the square to David's side.

22. The Triumphant Return

Captain Mott called his little army of fifteen to a halt by a clear running brook on the outskirts of the village of Sandisfield.

"Let's look smart," he said. "Use the brook to wash up. This is our last town before we split up."

David, John and Peter splashed water on their faces, slapped their breeches to dislodge the road dust and sauntered over to the shade of a giant maple. Spring was turning to summer and they were grateful for shelter from the sun.

"Peter, how about getting your fife and trying 'Yankee Doodle' again." David suggested. "You were a little ragged when we passed through that last village."

"We'll make an American of you, yet," John added with a laugh.

"How do you know I want to be an American?" Peter said, fishing his fife from a pocket of his faded red military jacket. "After all, I was a British soldier only a couple weeks ago. The only reason I consented to play 'Yankee Doodle' is that it was originally an English tune. I think of the English meaning when I play it, not the American."

"I don't believe it," David said. "You talk like an American already. When we passed through Skenesborough you saw Colonel Skene's stone mansion on the hill overlooking the village. You said it reminded you of your village in England where the squire ruled the town and collected high rents from everyone. You were glad Colonel Allen made prisoners of all the Tories there."

Peter blew an experimental note or two on his fife and said nothing. Fingering the instrument he launched into "Yankee Doodle." John held his hands to his ears in mock agony.

Captain Mott strolled over. "You're getting quite good, Peter. We'll be proud of you as we march through the last village."

Mott walked out to the dusty road and called the men together. "After this village you Salisbury men will split off for home and we'll head for Simsbury and Hartford. Let's put on a good show. Fall in!"

David unfolded a flag from his pack. He admired the blue field with the green pine tree in the corner and the red cross of St. George. The Pittsfield man who gave it to him said he had seen a flag like this at Lexington, the pine tree standing for the New England colonies. He had several made up and insisted that David take one, having heard what he had done at Ticonderoga.

John unhitched an old drum from his pack. He had found it in Skenesborough. Peter held his fife ready.

The boys moved to the head of the column, David tying the flag to a stick he had found. Captain Mott, Noah, Elisha and Levi Allen came next, followed by the men from Salisbury and Hartford, muskets on right shoulder.

"Look sharp!" Mott commanded as the little army marched to the rolling beat of John's drum.

Ahead, the white steeple of the village church was just visible over the trees. So far, they had been given a royal welcome in every town. News of their victory at Ticonderoga had spread before them.

Around the bend, the view of the little Western Massachusetts settlement unfolded. The village green was dominated by a small white church and flanked by a smithy, tavern and a dozen unpainted wooden houses.

Already the beat of John's drum was drawing the villagers from their homes and out of the tavern. Peter struck up "Yankee Doodle" on his fife and David straightened out the flag.

"Be ye from Ticonderoga?" an old man called. Captain Mott nodded.

"Roll out a barrel of cider!" someone shouted as the villagers crowded around, congratulating the soldiers on their victory.

A little boy trotted up to David, his eyes wide and wondering. He looked up and said, "Did you shoot any British soldiers?"

Startled, David looked down and rumpled the youngster's curly head. "No, but I brought one home." He pointed to Peter.

The boy tugged at Peter's sleeve. "Are you really a British soldier?" he asked, his eyes examining Peter from head to toe as if Peter might be some strange beast.

Peter squatted down and faced the youngster with a serious expression. "I'm not a soldier anymore. And, yes, I'm British, but most of the people in your village were British back through their grandfathers. They're Americans now and so am I."

David and John exchanged happy smiles.

The militiamen squatted on the green as the townsfolk plied them with food, drink and a hundred different questions about Ticonderoga. It was midafternoon before Captain Mott was able to get his little band on the road again.

On the march out of town David was saddened at the

thought of leaving John. He had grown very fond of John's dry humor, his bold, adventuresome spirit and his loyal companionship. He wished Simsbury and Salisbury weren't 30 miles apart.

Offsetting the sadness of parting was the happy knowledge that he would have Peter with him in Simsbury. Peter would love the big house by the river, the great meadows and the wonderful climb up the mountain to King Philip's cave.

His thoughts turned to cousin Matt with his devilish schemes and shy little Roxy, the only one who really appreciated his sketches of flowers. And won't Matt be bug-eyed when he finds he's really brought home a British soldier!

David's reverie was interrupted by Captain Mott's command to stop. Here was the crossroad where John and the Salisbury men must break off for home.

John grabbed David's arm, the boys struggled for words.

"You've got to come to Simsbury after the first haying," David pleaded.

"I'll be there," John vowed, "and I'll expect you in the fall for hunting along the Housatonnuck River."

John gave Peter a friendly slap. "You, too," he said and turned on his heel and followed the Salisbury contingent west.

David stood silent, watching the Salisbury group march down the road and out of sight around a bend. On impulse he threw back his head and let out the high-pitched call of the Great Horned Owl.

He listened. Back came John's answering owl call, distant but clear. It meant friendship and adventures shared and a pledge to meet again.

ABOUT THE AUTHOR

This is Mr. Fisher's first major work, although he has previously been published in *Boys' Life Magazine.* His interest both in young people and in history is evident in his many activities. He has been a leader in scouting and YMCA activities in Connecticut for the past 14 years. With his wife, he has led many Explorer Scout and Senior Girl Scout cycling and skiing trips. A resident of Simsbury, Connecticut, where *A Spy at Ticonderoga* originates, Mr. Fisher is a director of the Simsbury Historical Society and is currently heading the American Revolution Bicentennial Project to build an Indian village in Simsbury.